CHARISMA CHECK

Table Topped 2

Alex Silver

CONTENTS

Title Page
Copyright 1
Blurb 2
Chapter 1 3
Chapter 2 9
Chapter 3 19
Chapter 4 22
Chapter 5 42
Chapter 6 45
Chapter 7 52
Chapter 8 58
Chapter 9 63
Chapter 10 76
Chapter 11 83
Chapter 12 94
Chapter 13 100
Chapter 14 111
Chapter 15 126

Chapter 16 130
Chapter 17 137
Chapter 18 145
Chapter 19 153
Chapter 20 161
Chapter 21 172
Chapter 22 178
Chapter 23 182
Chapter 24 190
Chapter 25 195
Chapter 26 202
Chapter 27 210
Chapter 28 214
Chapter 29 220
Chapter 30 227
Chapter 31 235
About the Author 243
Table Topped Series 245
Hauntastic Haunts Series 248
Psions of SPIRE Series 252

COPYRIGHT

This is a work of fiction. Names, characters, places, and incidents either are the product of the author's imagination or are used fictitiously. Any resemblance to actual persons, living or dead, events, or locales is entirely coincidental. All registered trademarks are the property of their owners.

ISBN (print): 978-1-7773563-5-4
ISBN (ebook): 978-1-7773563-6-1

BLURB

Gui's the best friend I ever had. I love him like a brother, too bad I'm falling for *his* little brother.

Jude is a walking talking temptation, everything I never let myself want. He's sweet as chocolate, wickedly funny, and he gets me. The sex, well, it's worth a repeat and that's something I never do.

When he visited Gui, I thought I could settle for a one night stand, but then Jude moves to my city to work at my studio. Gui gets him to join my gaming group and suddenly he's all I see. Now Jude's looking at me with hearts in his eyes and I'm terrified that I'm going to break his heart.

Charisma Check is the second M/M romance in the Table Topped series. It features Jude, a hopeless romantic with diabetes who makes animation and Theo, a commitment-phobic trans man with depression who runs tabletop games for his friends.

CW: for severe depression, gender dysphoria, mention of past suicidality, surgical recovery, injection medications/needles (insulin dependent diabetes)

CHAPTER 1

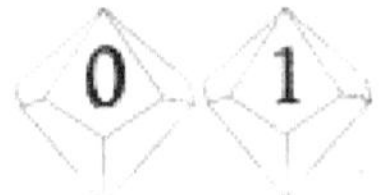

New Year's Eve
Jude

"Come on, Paz, didn't your man ever tell you about everyone's favorite animation principle?" Theo jokes as he tries to convince my brother and his boyfriend to go dancing with us. All their other friends have already left the game day that Gui hosted earlier to attend various New Year's celebrations.

I hope Theo's wheedling works, because much as I love Gui, we've spent most of my visit inside the apartment and I feel like a major third wheel. To be fair, his relationship with Paz is still new and shiny. If the sounds Gui tries to muffle after they go to bed are anything to judge by, Gui is one lucky bastard.

"Antici—" Theo says, and I lean in closer to him as he cackles.

"—pation, you jerk," Gui finishes the word, elbowing his neon orange-haired best friend. I duck my head to avoid staring at Theo. There's just something about him that makes it hard to tear my eyes away.

"That's my point!" Theo says. "Leave them hanging and they're sure to come back for more. Come out dancing, let the anticipation build for a few hours, and I guarantee you'll thank me when you get home. And I bet baby bro will thank me, too," Theo winks at me and nudges his foot against mine.

"Dude! Jude's off limits, Theo," Gui shoves his friend. "No screwing around with my baby brother."

"Hey! I'm right here," I point out, annoyed that Gui is pulling the big brother card and acting like I'm some little kid. I might have been fifteen when he left home and moved to Canada, but I've grown up in the past five years. I know Gui is just being protective, and I understand why.

According to Gui, Theo doesn't do relationships. In the years he and Gui have been friends, Theo hasn't been in a single actual relationship. I know this because Gui took me aside before Theo came over and warned me that Theo is a major flirt.

Gui knows me as the silly little cousin his parents adopted who watched too many rom-coms and dreamed about love. Love like my parents had. So big it makes the entire world look brighter until you can't live without it. Heck, my first attempt at creating animation was a stop motion wedding between two of my action figures. I'm a textbook hopeless romantic. I have no business getting involved with a player. Even an adorkable one who makes my heart flutter when he smiles at me.

"I can see that," Theo agrees with a flirty smile. His tone makes me think he not only sees me, he *likes* what he sees. "Calm your pearl clutching, G. I just meant Jude might like to get out and see the nightlife if you've kept him stuck in your love nest all week."

"He's underage," Gui snaps, and I don't miss the warning look he shoots at Theo. It's the same one his mom uses when she's telling us to behave or else. My mom had that same stern look, and my heart aches a little at the reminder.

Theo heaves a theatrical sigh, throwing his hands in the air and then landing one on my shoulder. "You're eighteen?" Theo asks me.

Gui scowls.

"Twenty," I say, jutting out my chin defiantly at my brother's overprotectiveness.

"Well, you're in luck. The drinking age is nineteen in BC. All the more reason to make the most of your visit, am I right?" Theo jostles me.

"I'm game," I agree with a smile.

"Great, that's settled! Party time. G, Jude and I are hitting Davie Street. Are you and your man joining us or being boring old coupled-off losers?" Theo stands and offers me his hand. I take it and he hauls me to my feet, his grip lingering just a moment too long. He gives me a soft smile, which I return.

"Can't. Paz has to work early," Gui says. Pascal kisses Gui's cheek.

"We could go for an hour or two. Or you can go without me," Pascal offers. But Gui is already shaking his head. "Nah, I don't want to wake you up in the middle of the night stumbling in drunk, it's fine. We can celebrate the new year here and go clubbing with Theo next week when you have Saturday off."

"I'm going to hold you to that." Theo points at my brother.

"If it'll be a problem for Paz, I don't have to go," I say,

feeling bad. Still, I really hope he won't take me up on the offer to skip the night out on the town.

"Go. It's fine, Jude," Paz waves me off, "You should have fun while you're in town."

Gui sighs. "Are you sure you'll be okay, Jude?"

"Yeah, bro, chill. Despite being your kid brother, I'm not an actual child," I assure him.

"You have your key, testing supplies, your passport card, and your phone?" Gui checks. I tried picking up beer the other day with my Cali driver's license, and they wanted to see my passport instead. So I've got my passport card tucked inside my phone case now. The actual passport is safely stowed with my suitcase.

"Yep," I agree, patting my pocket. Since Gui is off work for the week, he lent me his key while I'm visiting. He reasoned that he'd be with either me or Paz so he doesn't need it. The backpack with my meds and test kit is on a hook by the door, so I'll grab it as we leave.

"Stick close to Theo. Call if you need me for any reason, got it?" Gui says, going full-on overprotective big brother mode.

"Yes, Dad," I roll my eyes at him.

"We'll be fine, G." Theo takes my hand and leads me toward the door, with a shimmy in his step. "I'll show Jude a good time and deliver him home without a scratch on him and most of his innocence intact."

"You'd better, Theo," Gui calls after us.

"Cross my heart. Cheers," Theo waves away Gui's concerns and blows my brother a kiss. It's ridiculous and I can't help laughing at Theo's antics. He catches my eye and winks at me. "We'll be out late, at least until the balls drop." Theo waggles his eyebrows. Gui groans as I laugh at the terrible joke. "Don't wait up," Theo singsongs.

Then we're out the door. I shoulder my bag as Theo slings an arm around my shoulders, asking what kind of music I like and if I have a favorite drink. Just like that, I'm caught up in a whirlwind of excited banter about the best clubs to pull and where to go for dancing vs entertainment.

We hop on a bus that takes us over a bridge toward downtown, and I'm struck again by all the nature in this city. From the winter barren beaches near Gui's place, to the trees around Stanley Park, and the mountains and ocean all around us. It's a far cry from the desert and asphalt vistas I'm used to in the outskirts of LA.

"So, are you looking to get laid or just drink and dance?" Theo asks me casually and I'm left staring at him. He lets our thighs brush as we sit side-by-side and I'm not sure if he's propositioning me, or offering to help me pick up a guy.

"Um, why?" I ask.

Theo laughs. "So I can decide where to take you, Jude."

"Oh. Right. I enjoy dancing. I'm not as good at it as Gui, but we visit with his dad's family enough that I learned."

"*His* dad? Oh, right, Gui's parents adopted you, right?"

"Yeah. My folks died when I was eleven. Aunt Mere and Tio Carlo took me in. Guillermo and I were close before, but since then, he's been my brother in every way that counts."

"But his parents aren't your parents?" Theo asks with a shrewd look.

"They are," I say, but that isn't the entire story. Theo seems like someone who might understand, so I just blurt it all out. "But it feels wrong to call someone else Mom and Dad. When I'm talking *to* them, I call them Mamá and Papá, same as Gui, but when I talk *about* them to other people, it's Aunt Mere and Tio Carlo." I shrug, not sure how we got from picking a club to me emotionally vomiting all over my brother's best friend. But Theo just smiles at me and puts a hand on my thigh.

"Whatever you call them, it sounds like you have a loving family," Theo says with a soft smile.

"I do. What about you?" I ask.

"My fam? They're great. If you move out here for work, I'll take you and Gui up north to meet them. Blow your Cali-boy mind with all the snow." Theo gives me a flirty wink, then he pats my leg and reaches for the pull to stop the bus. "Come on, this is our stop, I'm taking you dancing."

CHAPTER 2

0 2

Theo

Taking Gui's baby brother dancing was a stupid, impulsive decision. It's not my fault Jude's fucking adorable. I know damn well Gui kept him cooped up with his hearts and rainbows new love all week, so the kid deserves a good time.

That good time should not include my dick. But as he rubs his sexy little ass against me on the dance floor, I am hard-pressed to remember why that's such a terrible idea. Maybe I'd have an easier time remembering if one-hour-ago-Theo hadn't broken the ice by loosening the kid up with shots. Now I've got my arms full of a sexy, writhing, tipsy Jude as he gyrates to the music. He wasn't lying about enjoying dancing. Or not being as coordinated as Gui. I might not have slept with my bestie, but I've danced with the guy. Paz is missing out by not coming with us tonight. Then again, Paz is probably getting laid right now. I need to stop thinking about Gui having sex when I'm feeling up his baby brother in a packed dance club.

Jude spins to face me, he loops his arms around my neck and leans in close. For a second, I think he's going to kiss me. Instead, he presses his mouth to my ear and murmurs, "I gotta pee."

"Want company?" I joke. And the heat in his eyes screams bad idea. Such a bad idea. This time Jude's lips do press against my mouth in a sloppy, boozy kiss. He plasters his body against me and I can feel the hard line of his dick pressed against me.

"Scratch that, think you can hold it long enough to piss at my place?" I offer. Because I am going to make a terrible decision, but I won't do it in a club washroom. Standards, right? Jude deserves better than a fumble in a toilet stall.

"How far away is it?" Jude asks, biting his lip.

"Not far, come on." I take his hand and lead him out of the club. We only stop to collect our jackets and Jude's bag before I'm leading him outside and down the street. I picked a place close to my apartment tonight, so it's a fast walk. That's not ideal. A longer walk might give us both a chance to cool off and make better choices.

Jude hangs on me as I dig out my keys. He presses more sloppy kisses to my neck and I wonder what he's like when he isn't drunk and if he's sober enough to agree to this. Am I really going to send him home to his brother drunk and freshly fucked?

"Wait." I put a hand on his chest, pushing him away.

"What?" Jude blinks at me, then his face falls. "Oh, shit. Sorry. You're not into me?" He takes a step back, almost tripping down the single step up to the door. I reach out and grab his arm to steady him. "Sorry," he repeats.

"Hey, no. I'm into you, Jude. I just need to know how drunk you are before this goes any further."

Jude licks his lips. I curse the Theo of three seconds ago because if he wasn't a cock-blocking wanker, I could be the one licking those pretty lips.

"Sheesh, I only had those three shots over an hour ago, same as you. I'm buzzed, but I know what I'm doing," Jude says, fisting his hands at his sides. His jaw clenches and there's fire in his dark eyes. I know I've fucked this up. I run a hand through my hair.

"The fact Gui would kill me if I took advantage of you, aside. I'm not a total asshole. If you aren't enthusiastically on board without being impaired, then I don't want to sleep with you."

"I'm not impaired. You act like I've never had a drink before. I just finished an animation internship. Do you honestly think this is my first night out, Theo? If you took me back here instead of to the club in the first place, I'd still want to kiss you. And I'd be a lot less horny for this argument."

I groan. "Me too. I'm an idiot. Still want to come inside? I can call you a cab."

"I don't want a taxi—I want you," Jude stomps his foot and it's cute as hell. He's hot and I'm horny. "And maybe your bathroom?" he adds, shuffling his feet a bit. "I wasn't lying about having to pee."

"Okay," I concede.

I'm not about to argue my way out of a good time. Jude doesn't seem too drunk to decide. We've both had the same amount and, yeah, I can feel the buzz, but I'm not wasted. I take his hand and lead him inside, shushing him as we stumble through the dark living room and down the hall to the washroom. "Your throne awaits." I gesture for him to go ahead. "My room's at the end of the hall. Come find me when you're done." I leave him to it, not wanting to creep him out by hovering near the door while he empties his bladder.

My tiny bedroom in the back barely accommodates my full-sized bed. I have to climb across the mattress to get to the closet, that's how cramped it is. I'm pretty sure this room started life as a utility space or a closet. It's jammed in between the washroom and an external wall, meaning my walls don't have immediate neighbors, unlike my four roommates. Jude and I should have privacy.

I flop onto my pillows to wait for him. A few moments pass and I'm wondering if he's having second thoughts. Then Jude stands in the doorway, staring at the bed. I sit up and grab his hand to give him a gentle tug forward. "Sorry, not enough room to shut the door unless you sit," I explain. The joys of Vancouver housing. Astronomical rent, itty-bitty living space, but I wouldn't want to live anywhere else.

"Tight fit," Jude observes, perching on the edge of my bed. I shut the door and lean closer to give him a tender kiss.

"That's what he said," I smirk at him and he stifles a laugh. "Or at least, I hope you'll be saying that. Want to fuck me, Jude?"

"Oh, um, yeah? Like... huh, I thought you were kind of more toppy. Sorry, tell me if I'm being super awkward, but like, which hole?"

Jude's flustered expression is almost cute enough to make up for the awkwardness of his question. I know that Gui mentioned I'm trans before I ever met the kid. Gui and I have been friends a long time, while this is the first time I've met his family in person, I know we've both heard plenty about each other through him. Besides, I'm pretty open about being trans. So of course Jude knows. If he'd asked me about my junk over pizza, that might be weird. In this context, figuring out which one of us is putting on the condom, it's more than reasonable to ask.

"Oh, I can be plenty toppy. I'm more in the mood to get fucked tonight," I reply as I knee-walk across the mattress to grab the condoms and lube from the top of my closet. "As to how, I'm not picky, but stick to calling it a hole, 'kay? No cutesy nicknames or anatomical references. If you have to differentiate, front or back works. And if you want to switch it up, I'm cool with that, but don't go from back to front." I hand him the condom.

"Right. Okay. Um." Jude just stares at the foil packet in his hand.

I get a sinking feeling as it occurs to me I might be on the verge of deflowering my bestie's brother, if he's this awkward about what goes where. "Babe, it's not rocket science. Just roll that on and stick your dick in me." I lean in to kiss him, hoping to take any sting out of the words and stop him from overthinking it. Jude won't meet my eyes, and I consider just leaving it at making out. We can get off without penetration if he's not into it.

"Sure, okay. Sorry. I'm being weird," Jude apologizes, licking his pretty lips. He shakes his head.

"It's fine," I kiss him again to get us both back in the mood. Jude sighs into my mouth, his body relaxes against mine. I delight in making him lose himself in the way our mouths move together. I reach for his fly. Jude moans when I pull his dick out, giving him a gentle tug. He's not circumcised and his foreskin lets my hand glide in a smooth stroke along his length, slicked by his pre-cum. I'm struck with a moment's pure envy at how his body works. I shove that thought ruthlessly away. Dysphoria is a bitch; one I'm not inviting along for a threesome.

Jude humps into my hand, reminding me I'm having sex with a cute guy. That helps me refocus on him. I break off the kiss to smirk at Jude; I like him needy and moaning. "If you're not into penetration, I can jerk you off instead," I offer.

"I'm into it," Jude replies, voice all breathy with pleasure as I continue to jerk him in slow strokes. Okay, cool, so far so good. I take the condom from him with my free hand and give up my grip on his dick to tear open the wrapper and roll the thin latex onto him.

"Is there a but coming there?" I ask when he just stares at me.

"Well, I hope you let me come in your butt," Jude says in a joke worthy of my juvenile sense of humor. I throw my head back and laugh.

"Sure. I am more than happy to accommodate that request," I agree, turning and wriggling out of my pants. I leave my underwear on. As much as he's hot and I'm into this, I need the reassuring bulge of my packer right now. I assume the position on all fours and reach behind me to pull my tight briefs aside and give him access. "Which hole am I lubing up for you, babe?"

"Um, is one better for you?" Jude asks. It's a valid question that I am in no mood to get into.

"Depends on my mood. I'm not having the best dysphoria day, so the back hole sounds better right now, if that's cool?"

"Yeah. Of course. Whatever you want," Jude nods. I could kiss his cute face again. Instead, I finger my ass for him, shoving two fingers inside. Jude stares in appreciation.

"You can touch me," I prompt him when he doesn't make any move to get to the good stuff.

Jude shakes himself. "Sorry, not used to topping."

"Do you not like it?" I ask, prepared to pivot to something else.

"I do. Just, I mean, I think I will."

I suppress a groan. "Am I your first time topping, baby?" I ask, voice soft.

He gives a sharp nod, catching his lip between his teeth. It's cute that he's nervous to admit it.

"Okay. Do you want this?" I check.

He nods again. "Yes."

"Then take your time, but I'm good to go when you're ready, just line up and push against my rim. I was fooling around with a toy earlier, so I should be nice and open for you."

Jude's hand on my hip is tentative, but then he guides his dick to my hole and I moan as he presses into my body. There is nothing so hot as letting a guy fuck me with my underwear still on. It makes me feel sexy and desired. Like he's so into me, he can't wait long enough to take them off. And it lets me jerk my packer instead of touching my junk when I'm in a mood like tonight. I press the semi-soft silicone against myself as I bear down to help Jude get inside me.

He's more gentle than I prefer. Too sweet for me. But I can't seem to resist his charms.

"This okay?" he asks as he inches his way into my body.

"Yeah, baby," I agree. "You can go a bit harder, I like it rough."

"How rough?" Jude asks, easing back, then rocking into

me.

"Like, fuck me into the mattress. Pin me down and make me forget my name?"

"Yeah?" His voice cracks a little and reminds me forcefully that he's Gui's kid brother and I'm an absolute wanker for doing this with him. Except Jude is an adult, and it would be shitty of me to act like he isn't capable of deciding what he wants. Even if I know this is a mistake.

"Yeah. I'll tell you if you're hurting me or anything. It's just sex."

"Okay," Jude agrees. Then he gets a firmer grip on me and takes me at my word. Gone is the timid boy getting his dick inside someone for the first time. He holds me tight and nudges my legs apart further, his fingers dig into my ass, stinging just enough to make me rock back into him.

"Ngh," I cry out, then moan encouragement when he hesitates at the sound. "Yeah just like that."

Jude takes my cue, adjusts his angle and slams into me. Now we're talking. He lets go and fucks me hard enough to make my headboard thump against the wall on each thrust. When it gets louder, he slows his pace.

"Don't slow down," I demand, "Exterior wall, it's fine."

Jude redoubles his efforts, fucking me hard enough that he shoves me forward into the pillows. I'm grinding against the soft base of the packer as I squeeze the dick in my pants like it might suddenly grow nerves if I focus on it hard enough. Fuck.

"Harder, Jude, please," I beg, needing the pleasure-pain of his thrusts to drown out everything else.

"I'm trying," Jude groans. He grabs my underwear to pull my ass up higher. The fabric bites into my skin deliciously, as he shifts on the bed to get better leverage and gives me his all.

"Pull my hair," I order him. Jude complies, giving me a good yank that forces me back onto his dick at an angle that feels like he's fucking against my junk from the inside. "Oh, fuck, yes. Just like that, babe."

It's not perfect and I'm not in the best head space, but it's good. And even when he's as rough as I demand of him, Jude has a sweetness to him. His palm splayed over my ass conveys tenderness, even as he does his level best to split me open with his dick. He drives in deep and I can feel how close he is from his erratic rhythm and heavy breathing. I want him to mark me, slap my ass or something, that bit more to tip me over the edge.

"I'm close, Theo," Jude groans, giving my hair a sharp jerk and digging his blunt nails into my ass. Oh, yes, that's what I needed.

"Babe, yes, fuck," I buck back against him in frantic jerks as my dick pulses and all my core muscles clench around him.

"You're so tight, Theo. God, I can't..." then Jude drives in deep, shoving me down into the mattress as he rides out his own orgasm, buried as deep inside me as he can get. Yeah, I'd be lying if I said I didn't like his weight pressing me into the sheets and how he clings to me afterward. Jude kisses my shoulders and ruts out the aftershocks like I'm more than a quick and dirty hookup. Like he wants to cling to the connection between us until his cock is too soft to stay inside me. He pulls out and deals with the condom.

"Just tie it off and toss it on the floor for later," I mumble into the pillows when he hesitates. I can't tell if he's unsure what to do with it or wondering if he should leave. He does as instructed and I pull him down to snuggle. I'm almost asleep when he wriggles away.

"It's late," he says, glancing at my alarm clock. It's a little past midnight and the thought that we started off the new year with a bang makes me smile.

"What?" He gives me a quizzical look.

"Just thinking that so far, it's a pretty fucking happy new year," I wink, and tug him toward me for a kiss.

"Mm. Happy new year to us," he says when he pulls away. Then he sighs and adds, "I should head back to Gui's."

"You can stay the night," I offer. I enjoy sleeping next to a warm body, and Jude is a perfect fit against me. I'm not good at being alone, even if I do kick out most of my hook-ups first thing the morning after. "You can tell Gui you crashed on my couch so you wouldn't wake Paz," I add when he hesitates to reply.

"Okay," he agrees. Jude snuggles into me, his breath warm on my neck, his leg thrown over my hips so I can feel his soft dick against me. I appreciate having him wrapped around me like this. No need to delve into the guilty feeling that I'm crossing yet another line with Jude. He's an adult, and Gui has no right to tell either of us who we can fuck or sleep with. It's not like either of us is going to catch feelings after one night together. Besides, Jude lives half a continent away in another country, so this is just one night. Gui mentioned something about him moving, but what are the odds he'll follow through on moving to a new country?

CHAPTER 3

0 3

March
Jude

It's not like I've spent the past few months pining over Theo or anything. I don't expect a marriage proposal just because he let me sleep over, but it would be nice if he acknowledged that we fucked. I haven't mentioned what happened to Gui. He will freak if he learns I hooked up with his friend.

It's not like it meant anything. Not to Theo. I bet it sucked for him, since I'd never topped before. It means nothing that I shared a first with him. It's not like I'm still hung up on the first guy I kissed, or the first boyfriend I fooled around with. I can do casual; just two guys getting off together. Right?

Except I still have a major crush on Theo. Now that I work with him, I keep seeing him around the studio. I live with his best friend, so it's not like I can avoid him until my crush fades. As if that isn't bad enough, Gui seems determined to have me join their gaming group. Where I can spend hours in the same room as Theo, interacting with him, watching him. Flirting.

Despite his radio silence after our night together, I still want him. I'd woken up alone in his tiny bedroom to a note that he'd gone to get us coffee and bagels. I'd been groggy, my sugar low from the sugarfree shots of booze I'd consumed the night before. Alcohol fucked with my sugars, but I knew my limits. When Theo returned, it was like the man who cuddled with me after sex had disappeared. No more comfortable touches or soft smiles. He didn't comment on my insulin when I dosed myself before we ate, but he side-eyed the needle. Breakfast passed in awkward silence. Theo apologized when he noticed I wasn't drinking the coffee, and I admitted to not being a coffee person. Caffeine messes with my sugar too, and I don't like it enough to bother with the fluctuations. That admission led to an awkward silence. Then I went home and lied to my brother about sleeping on Theo's couch.

Gui gave me that big brother look, like he could search my soul and detect any lies. I held firm to my story until he shook his head and accepted my words at face value. When I called after I got home from Vancouver, I didn't ask about Theo. Gui didn't mention him to me unprompted.

It wasn't like I had time to mope about things not working out differently. I'd known going in that Theo didn't do romance. And a few weeks after my return to California, I got offered my dream job at Eye-On. My contract started when the work on *Day Dreamer 2* was ramping up. Since the studio shuffled people off of *Battle Fox*, they had openings on both projects. I only had a few weeks to figure out my part of the visa paperwork. An international move came with a ton of details to iron out. Everything from housing to making a plan for continuity of my healthcare. That was all piled on top of stressing over my first real grown-up job. So I was too busy to get hung up on a guy.

Now though, without the entire west coast separating us, I am stressing about it. I haven't seen Theo more than in passing, yet. Too busy settling into my new routine.

I'm working on crowd animations for *Battle Fox*. Stuff that will barely be noticeable in the backgrounds, if I do my job right. I have to work faster and to a higher quality than I'm used to from school, though. My first few weeks living with Gui and Paz passed uneventfully. I invested in rechargeable batteries for my noise canceling headphones. Best investment I'd made, since I use them for work and drowning out my brother's sex sounds. I work late a lot, too. That's something I expected coming into the industry from talking with Gui and my internship.

Tonight I need to wrap up on time. It's game night, and I promised Gui I'd play, since they're down a group member. I've never played VentureQuest. Gui claims it's like the *Call of Cthulhu* games he ran when we were younger. So if it wasn't for seeing Theo again, I'd be all over the chance to make new friends in the city. As it stands, I'm an anxious wreck about the game night. I'm also concerned about how Gui will react if I let on that anything weird happened between Theo and me. The last thing I want is to fuck up their friendship over my stupid decision to sleep with a guy I always knew wasn't into me romantically.

CHAPTER 4

Theo

Game night has arrived at last, and I am more than ready to get it on. The game, I mean. Not my libido. That can wait. I've been planning this new campaign for months while production ramps up for Day Dreamer 2. I dump my stuff on the table in the conference room I reserve every other Friday night.

My entire gaming group works at Eye-On Games. The studio is pretty casual, no one cares if we hang out after hours so long as we aren't disruptive to anyone working late. And don't forget to set the alarm before we leave. I only forgot once. And Gui mentioned something that reminded me to go back and punch in the code before we even made it all the way to the bar for post-game drinks. So it doesn't *really* count. No matter how much the gang likes to razz me about it. At least one of them always sticks around to remind me now, since I'm the slowest to pack up and leave.

"Is everybody ready?" I ask. I'm still organizing my stuff and getting my laptop set up, so I can reference my notes. The rulebook PDFs, game details, copies of everyone's character sheets, and anything else that comes up. Errol revels in keeping me on my toes, but I'm ready for him.

"Let's do this." Gui grins at me.

"Heck, yes, bring it on," Laura agrees.

"The sooner you do the intro, the sooner we can play," Errol says, somewhere between bored and amused. Jude and Max just kind of smile and nod. They're new to the group, so I'm not sure how they'll fit with our dynamic yet. I hope at least one of them sticks around to replace Pia while they're out on mat leave.

It's a little awkward that Gui invited Jude to join our group. He started working with us a few weeks ago, and that spark I felt with him on New Year's hasn't gone away. I don't do repeats. Let alone dating. So I've been avoiding Jude.

That can't last when he lives with Gui. Another reason you don't screw around with your best friend's brother. Past Theo is a jerk for putting me in this situation. Although, Jude playing with us could be a perfect opportunity to rip the Bandaid off and get over being hung up on the guy. Get to know him as a friend. There is just something intriguing about him.

I find it adorable how excited he is to be working at Eye-On Games. Like it's so cool he's here and he's got these rose-tinted glasses about everything. Tonight he's wearing a studio branded hoodie that must be Gui's because he's swimming in the oversized garment. I think the studio name blazoned across his chest has a creepy stalker vibe. The company logo is neat, in a sinister sort of way. It reminds me of the eye of Sauron from the LOTR movies. I like to joke that Eye-On always has its eyes on you.

It's Jude's first adult job, not counting a student internship, and I kind of envy his optimism about our industry. To be fair, our job is pretty fucking cool. We make several popular fantasy adventure series. But it's not all sunshine and roses.

The rest of us, save Max, have been around longer, so we're a bit jaded about crazy hours, fickle contracts, and the need to move to where the work is. For now, Vancouver is enough of a hub that I'm lucky to live close to my family. That could change any time, though. Gui and Jude are from California, and even a few years ago there was plenty of work there. Now, it seems the industry is moving to places with better tax incentives.

Anyway. Gui is an animation supervisor. Jude's a brand new baby junior animator. Laura is a 3-D modeler. Pia does concept art when they aren't on leave. I'm a lighter. I take the stuff Laura and Pia create after Jude and Gui bring it to life and make it all shine. And I do it in the dark, it's a whole thing. We call our floor the cave, because it's easier to light a scene if you don't have competing light sources.

Errol is in production. Meaning his need to boss everyone around and penchant for rules policing serves him well. He makes sure we artists and the folks who do the programming all get our work in on time and the pipeline runs smoothly. He's good at it too.

Max is in production as well, but he's what we call a coffee peon. Or his actual title, a runner. As in, he runs to get things for the higher ups. And everyone is on a higher rung than the runner. He's paying his dues and hoping to earn a better position now that his foot is in the door.

The reason Max and Jude are here tonight is that Pia, one of our regulars, is planning to take the full seventeen weeks of paid parental leave they get after giving birth in December, if not the entire year. So, that's the gang. We meet every other Friday for our game sessions, when I take my friends on an adventure to another world. One where we can be anything, or anyone. Even dragons.

I meet everyone's eyes, then launch into the backstory for the campaign.

Legend has it the war between Ethar and Laud began in time immemorial. That's a long time for a dragon. Many human lifetimes. Etharians hold that a vast human horde besieged their great Citadel of Dragonis. A place of great importance to dragonkind, for nigh on a year before the Laudan forces burned the temple and its denizens to ash. The Laudan side claims the attack was justified since the dragons stole a relic of great cultural importance to the Laudan royal family.

Laudans only know where their side lays the blame for the conflict, they have no interest in dragon propaganda. No dragon has heard the Laudan side of the story. No dragon would deign to listen to a Laudan's version of events either.

The war raged bloody and brutal between the two nations. The frail human warriors fell easily to the dragon forces. However, though they are a long-lived and hardy people, the dragons have few children and take centuries to mature. Lifetimes of war between the neighboring countries took their toll, and both nations were in danger of collapse.

It came to a head during the reign of the human king, Wendal I, thereafter known as Wendal Paxtus. As with all the kings and queens before him, Wendal was mage-born, having the longer lifespan of a dragon while appearing human. With this great age, he saw that continuing the war would mean the downfall of both peoples. Already, Laud's neighbors to the east had made incursions, taking lands along the border. And border patrols had spotted strange ships along the northern coast, perhaps scouting ahead for invaders from beyond the Sapphire Sea. Wendal realized his nation must make peace to survive.

In desperation, to preserve what remained of his kingdom after the unending war, King Wendal sent a delegation to meet with the leader of the Etharian dragons. They arrived at the border between Ethar and Laud, near the site of the destroyed citadel, unarmed and seeking peace.

The eldest among the dragons, their leader Great Wyrm Thernal, met with King Wendal. Thernal, too, had seen the devastation wrought on their people. They had received reports of warships to the north as well. And in their wisdom, the two leaders forged an alliance.

Laud and Ethar, once the bitterest of rivals, would now join forces and present the northern invaders with a united front. By land, by sea, and by air, they would repel the threat and then coexist in peace. To seal their agreement, the human forces joined with the dragons to rebuild the citadel. A shining beacon of peace between the two nations. The second seal on the treaty, as so often happens in these matters, was a betrothal between Thernal and Wendal's children.

The only problem was that Thernal's heir was yet an egg. So the hundred years betrothal began. Wendal sent the most beautiful of his children to tend to Thernal's clutch, so that the hatchling would know the voice of their betrothed. Legend has it, the dragon singers of Laud were later born of this child, the fiercest of the Laudan royal line. Each bonded to a dragon warrior from the shell to the grave.

Thernal's first clutch failed. Their second clutch produced a single hatchling. And while the hatchling was hearty and hale, Wendal's child grew old by the time the hatchling was mature enough to take a mate. The hatchling, called Prince Sythern, after the human title for their leaders, came to maturity many human generations later, during the reign of Wendal's mage-born heir, King Dalan III. When the Great Wyrm called upon King Dalan to honor his father's agreement, he sent his mage-born second son, Prince Tamsin, to wed the dragon prince. And so nigh on two centuries after the treaty signing, the second seal came to fruition in the union between Prince Tamsin and Lesser Wyrm Sythern.

"Ugh, gross, isn't that like bestiality?" Max interrupts me.

I heave a sigh. It's a minor miracle my players let me get as far as I did into the backstory. It would have been nice to finish with no interruptions for once.

New group of adventurers, new VentureQuest campaign. That's how I roll. Well, I let my players do most of the rolling, but the point stands. I want to immerse everyone in the story, especially the new players.

Jude is practically a tabletop virgin. I want to help him get into character by giving him a feel for the world that I spend my free time creating. I take my game master responsibilities seriously. As a GM, my goal is to give my players an epic experience at every session. Gotta keep them coming back for more.

"No, dragons are shapeshifters, right?" Laura asks, she looks to me for approval and I suppress an eye roll. Because I'm pretty sure the major source of lore where dragons are shifters features in romance novels. No shade, but I am not running that kind of campaign. Although the way Jude keeps glancing at me with his big doe eyes, I might consider it. *Bad Theo.* Gui's brother is off limits. If only my libido got that memo three months ago.

"Not in VQ 6.5," Errol, our resident rules policer chimes in. Great, I do not need Errol to go off on a tangent about variations in VentureQuest rules regarding dragons. Or worse, branching off into comparing their stats in every tabletop system on the market. And some that are off the market for good measure.

I glance at our newbies to gauge their reactions. I don't want them scared off during their first session. We already had to take a three-month hiatus after Pia left to tend to their spawn. Or her spawn. Pia prefers us to alternate pronouns for them, but they weren't as comfortable with she/her while pregnant. Now that Rain is a few months old and Pia is more comfortable with both again, I make a mental note to practice alternating again, and check in with her about how she's doing.

I have nothing against them taking parental leave to bond with the little crotch-goblin, in fact, I sort of like babies; as long as they're going home with someone else. My nephew Skyler's pretty rad. But Pia leaving the group means that our party lost its bard. Still, I can admit her baby is pretty cute, when the kid isn't screaming, puking or pooping.

Pia sent a picture to our group chat earlier this week of little Rain napping on a blanket on the ground with Pia's partners. Gregor and Emil are zonked out on either side of the tiny goober. Rain is as bald as Gregor and has a fistful Emil's hair in their hand.

At least Pia gave me enough notice to wrap up the campaign we were in the middle of before spraying me with amniotic fluid. That might be a slight exaggeration, but I will never let Pia live it down. With *Day Dreamer's* deadline and Pia's due date looming, we'd had to wrap up the campaign sooner than I'd planned. Hence the rather abrupt sacking of the citadel had spelled the end of our last adventure. The fact Bruce the paladin had kicked off the war between Ethar and Laud was neither here nor there.

The argument about whether dragons and humans can copulate is heating up, and has my newbies looking like a flight risk as they exchange uncomfortable glances.

"Dragons don't have sex for pleasure," I interject, hoping to shut down the argument. "It's part of why they have so few offspring."

"Are humans and dragons reproductively compatible?" Errol asks. "You know, since they are royalty and will both need heirs. Isn't forming family bonds half the point of that kind of treaty?"

"Does that mean they're ace?" Laura asks. Her mouth twists like she's tasted something sour. Her posture stiffens defensively. She's asexual and bi-romantic. My sister is aro and ace. And I'm pretty sure I remember Errol saying he's demi. So no, dragons aren't some mythical way of othering Laura, Errol, and Erin. Or non-binary people like Pia.

"No, but Tamsin is ace. The human prince," I say. "He and Sythern have a romantic relationship, despite it being arranged."

Laura nods, her face softening. "Cool."

Errol shakes his head. "Haven't we already established that human genders and sexualities don't apply to other sentient species?" He's right. That had been a huge debate when we played a sci-fi themed GURPS campaign a few years back. Errol and Gui had played aliens, each trying to outdo the other for being the least human-like. Pia had played a symbiote who had bonded with a pod of hosts of varying species amongst whom they could change at will as the circumstances dictated. That had made for interesting play mechanics and given Pia loads of backstory to experiment with.

"Yep," I agree. "These dragons are sexually monomorphic. They all have the same reproductive parts. Sex is a process for them to produce offspring. They exchange genetic material during an elaborate ritual group flight with magic. Then they lay eggs, which may or may not hatch. They mate or form romantic bonds for companionship and mutual gain. Gender, as a concept, is foreign to them. Most use neutral pronouns when speaking in human languages. Or they switch among them since they have a hard time grasping the nuances of the concept."

I didn't intend to discuss dragon gender identity or sexuality at our first session, but that's why I always plan out the whole backstory. So I can handle these random tangents the group has a knack for finding.

If I can rely upon my regulars for anything, it's that they will find the most random detail possible to fixate on. Errol revels in derailing a campaign if he can manage it. Errol frowns and I can see an argument forming as he opens his mouth, so I charge ahead to forestall him.

"Prince Sythern uses the human title since they took a human mate. And the masculine form, because patriarchy. Their dragon title is Lesser Wyrm Sythern, at least until they assume their parent's throne and become the Great Wyrm. Oh, and the dragons trace their lineage through the egg layer, because mating flights are big communal affairs. So they don't bother tracking the other genetic parent. Dragons and humans can't interbreed. As Sythern's mate, the dragons will consider prince Tamsin the co-parent of any children Sythern has. Tamsin's older brother, the crown prince, will carry on the human line of succession. Tamin and Sythern's heirs will be considered their cousins."

Errol looks satisfied with my answer and subsides.

"So, as I was saying, Prince Tamsin and Prince Sythern have a mating ceremony in Ethar and wed in Laud according to the traditions of both countries. They live in the Etharian capital. And the peace between Ethar and Laud continues to grant prosperity to both nations until —"

"Wait, wait, hold up, I just... did we start the war?" Errol asks.

"Yes," I snap. "When you sacked the citadel at the end of the last campaign, you started a war that almost destroyed Laud."

Errol fist-pumps and lets out a victorious whoop. "Score! I told you guys lawful good could wreak some serious unintended evil!"

"Lawful good for the evil win," Gui fist-bumps him.

Right. Our last campaign had turned into a race to the bottom between our rogue, played by Laura and Errol's paladin of light. They competed to see who would do more harm to the general good. Laura's rogue epitomized chaotic neutral greed, and she still did more good than the paladin. The best had been when Laura stole a key that ended up setting off an alarm spell. The alarm resulted in the city guard stopping an illegal smuggling ring from distributing tainted drugs that would have killed people. She just wanted the key on the off chance it might open a loot chest later. Nevermind she could pick locks.

In contrast, Errol's character, Bruce the paladin, was the one who set fire to the citadel full of innocent dragon monks. By his logic, since they were sheltering a criminal who had stolen Laud's crown jewels, they weren't on the side of good. Ergo they must be evil, and it was his duty to stop their wicked ways.

That was partly on me for not realizing just how powerful his one magical reward from earlier in the campaign could be in the wrong hands. A measly ring of summoning. I limited him in what he could summon and how long it lasted. But then he stacked some other effects on it with other quest rewards. He used it to call up an overpowered buffed up fire imp that obeyed his commands and rolled like a freaking god and nuked all my hard work.

Yeah, Errol likes to break things. Like my carefully constructed narratives. And the sweet final dungeon, complete with epic boss battle, that I had planned. And since they fulfilled the technical terms of their quest, the party got the hero treatment when they returned to Laud after the mission.

Hence this campaign was born. So Errol can see the consequences his thoughtless actions had on both Laud and Ethar. And setting this campaign hundreds of years in the future means that Bruce the paladin, bane of my existence as a GM, is long since dead and buried.

I've already given myself permission to pull a 'rocks fall, you die' if the bastard tries to return from the dead, too.

So. I've been told I get a teensy bit intense about my narrative. It's true. But in my defense, I work hard to craft the finer details that make the story come alive. I want my players to have fun. I love creating a story that has them leaving each session abuzz with excitement, but I don't like it when they break my toys, so to speak.

All the side chatter is losing Jude and Max's attention, so I pivot back to the topic at hand. "Right, so, to recap: our previous group of adventurers set fire to the citadel. That made them heros in Laud and villains in Ethar. And kicked off this massive war between the two countries. It's now a thousand years later. The war has been over for a century and we have Prince Tamsin and Lesser Wyrm Sythern settling into married life."

"Um, so, where does the role play come in?" Max asks, like a jerk.

Errol snorts. I pointedly ignore them both.

"Theo likes to get into the world building, let him talk." Gui hushes the newbie. Good. Gui always has my back. That's why he's the ideal best friend. I shoot him a thankful look and check my notes to make sure I get the next part just right. It's the opening scene of our new adventure and I want to get everything perfect.

"Questions before we start tonight's session?" I ask, arching a brow.

I wait a beat to give them time to speak up, then I set the scene.

"Prince Tamsin is in his rooms when the palace guard informs him that Sythern never returned from his morning flight. A few hours later, the Great Wyrm receives a note from human mercenaries claiming responsibility for kidnapping the heir to the dragons. They are demanding a ransom. As a dragon, Great Wyrm Thernal cannot set the precedent that their hoard is available for negotiations. Not even against the return of their most prized treasure, Sythern. So instead of paying, Thernal calls upon the treaty. They task Tamsin with assembling a team of the greatest heros in the realm to recover their stolen heir."

I pitch my voice in my best imitation of a dragon's low rumble as I speak for the ancient creature. "Thernal says, 'These villains demand I choose between the two things most precious to any dragon heart. I cannot bear to part with my hoard, and yet the thought of them harming Sythern is worse. We must find these villains and bring them to justice! I call upon you, Prince Tamsin, in honor of the agreement between our two peoples: you must rescue your mate. If any harm befalls them at the hands of human villains, it will surely mark the return to war between our two nations.' and Tamsin replies, 'I swear on my honor, I will see Sythern returned safe to my side, Great Wyrm." I pitch my voice higher for Tamsin. It's always fun to fool around with the various characters.

I rush out the last bit of introduction because if I let the gang get a word in, I'll lose my momentum. "So Tamsin vows to rescue the captured dragon prince, before the Great Wyrm and his gathered advisors. But he knows that not even a prince of two realms can undertake such a gallant quest on his own. He calls upon the greatest heroes of the realm to accompany him on his rescue mission. The five great heroes gather at the restored Citadel of Dragonis to begin their adventure."

"That's us, right?" Laura asks, fidgeting in her seat.

"Obviously," Errol says, idly stacking his dice.

"So, wait, the dragon got kidnapped by a bunch of humans?" Max crosses his arms, like he's too cool for this.

I want to roll my eyes, but I refrain. It's never a good idea to alienate the players. But I do not appreciate the interruption. I clear my throat.

"As I was saying... the heroes gather at the citadel," I say. I have all their character outlines in my notes so I can incorporate them and their motivations into this intro. My favorite thing about tabletop is collaborating to create the story. I love making an alternate reality with my friends. There was a time when in-game was the only place I truly felt like myself, and that same magic lives on whenever I run a game.

"First, Tamsin's childhood friend, knight commander Zelphod Beetlefeet. A human fighter proficient with swords, he is the leader of Tamsin's personal guard."

"I console my oldest friend and swear to help reunite Tamsin with his beloved dragon consort," Errol says for Zelphod.

Errol is trying his hand at a brute strength approach instead of min-maxing a more complex class this time. Although I can already see him eyeing levels of prestige classes to spice things up down the line.

I hope the simple human fighter role allows more room for our newbies to shine. In-game, Errol has a tendency to trample over others in his zeal to get things done sometimes.

"Then comes the mage-born dragon singer, Larris Lightwing, and her bonded dragon Pebbles," I say.

"Pebbles and I swear to bring Lesser Wyrm Sythern home unscathed. For our honor and the good of all Ethar," Laura says, in character. Oh, dear god, why do I let Laura name things? Who calls a fearsome dragon companion Pebbles?

Gui snorts at the name and shoots Laura a thumbs up. The dragon singer class is something we sort of cobbled together ourselves when Laura was making her character. Based on a druid crossed with a bard and a healthy splash of sorcerer.

I think it's going to turn out pretty cool. I just hope it balances alright without having to screw around with Pebbles's stats too much, since a dragon animal companion seems super overpowered. We'll see. I can always fudge numbers as needed to even out the difficulty.

"The third member to join the party is Carl. Carl is a ranger, looking to prove himself in the field," I intone.

"I long for the day when bards will sing of our daring deeds. If any task was ever worthy of immortalizing in song, surely it is saving the dragon heir," Gui proclaims. He grins at me. I definitely need to have a chat with the group about naming conventions in Ethar and Laud.

"Fourth to arrive is Maximus Powers, a sorcerer from the mysterious north. He agrees to join Tamsin on his quest for access to rare materials for his spells that he can only find in the citadel gardens," I say.

That would be Max. Errol recruited him for this campaign. I'm not sure how I feel about Max joining the group. So far, he rubs me the wrong way, but I'll reserve judgment. Errol's been taking him under his wing, so he can't be all bad.

I had to talk Max out of playing a wizard because I told Errol he couldn't play one for this campaign. And if I let Max do it, then Errol will grumble. Ain't nobody got time for that shit.

"I'm just here for the endangered botanicals," Max drawls.

"The last hero in our noble quest is a dragon monk from the citadel, Lyran. They've volunteered to join the team to protect Ethar and the citadel from the chaos that will no doubt ensue if the quest fails and harm befalls Sythern," I say. Last but not least, Jude.

It's weird to GM for a guy I want to flirt with, I've had sort of an unofficial rule about not fooling around within my gaming group. Screws up the dynamics when the relationship inevitably fails. Of course, that goes double with Jude, since a rift with him will hurt my friendship with Gui, too.

Too bad I can't shake the desire to make him laugh. Right. Jude, I might be staring at him. In my defense, he's adorkable. I like the way he smiles, all shy and sweet. And I like his face. Yep, definitely staring.

And the gang is staring back at me, all expectant. Shit, I lost my train of thought, where was I?

"So, we are all assembled with Prince Tamsin at the citadel?" Gui, bless him, takes pity and moves things along before the silence gets anymore awkward. He gives me a look that says he noticed my lapse and we will have words about it later. That's a problem for future Theo.

"Right, you're all meeting for the first time. Tamsin is assembling his team of heros in the temple's inner sanctum."

"You mean the nave?" Laura wrinkles her nose.

"That's for cathedrals," Errol corrects her.

"It's a large vaulted room with intricate carvings etched in the walls and ceiling after the dragon style of art. The head monk, Elder Yaren, has agreed to host the assembly and assist the team in gathering supplies," I describe the scene.

"Can I test charisma to see if he'll let me check out the temple gardens?" Max demands.

I suppress another eye roll. Great. Max isn't working out, I can tell already. I hate interpersonal conflict, but if he proves not to be a good fit, I'll have to handle it.

"Maximus attempts to persuade the elder to give him spell components," I rephrase his request for him through clenched teeth. I prefer for my players to delve into their roles, Max is going to kill my buzz. I roll a D20 and pretend to check a table. Sometimes I make up the result that best serves the narrative in cases like this. Other times, I really let the dice decide. But I never tell the crew about that to maintain my mystique.

"Elder Yaren is not impressed by the blatant attempt at personal gain. He says, 'Our order has already committed to provide everything that your party requires for returning our Lesser Wyrm to their rightful place. As such, you are welcome to restock your magical supplies from our gardens.' Yaren gestures toward the gardens. 'If you are successful, you brave heroes will have the gratitude of all Ethar.'"

"Thank you, Elder. Pebbles and I will never forget all you've done for us over the years. We will return triumphant, or not at all," Laura vows, speaking as Larris. Laura is always enthusiastic to go along with my narrative.

"The bards will sing of our deeds!" Gui jumps in as Carl. He's my rock. Got to love Gui.

"I, uh, will miss you Elder Yaren," Jude ducks his head, and it makes him ten times cuter. As roleplay goes, it's a smidge weak, but the guy is trying, and I can respect his efforts at RP.

"You will do us all proud, Lesser Lyran," I say in my best old man NPC voice. "You have earned the privilege of accompanying our Lesser Wyrm's consort on this quest through your dedication to the citadel and Ethar."

Jude's flush deepens. OMG, this guy is going to kill me. It's official, popping Jude's tabletop cherry is shaping up to be the most fun I've had in ages. Or maybe I need to get out more. Or get laid. It's been a bit of a dry spell since January. I've been busy. Not thinking about pretty dark eyes and gentle hands.

"Thank you Elder, I won't let you down," Jude replies solemnly.

"Wait, Errol didn't mention we have to talk in character. Is this a thing with you guys? And when do we get to the good stuff?" Max complains.

"Theo likes to focus on the roleplay," Errol says, in the same dry tone he might say 'Theo has a scat fetish.'

"No one is forcing you to be here," Gui says, eyes narrowing. His defense further cements his position as my best friend, he's always got my back.

"You are welcome to join another group, if you'd prefer to just roll dice and beat up bad guys or whatever," I say, feeling peevish.

"Theo is the GM, if you don't like his rules then don't play," Laura says. Good ol' loyal Laura.

"Whatever," Max grumbles, "I go out to the gardens to look for spell components."

"Prince Tamsin calls after Maximus, 'Before you go, I'd like to address my champions."

"Fine." Max sighs as he slumps sulkily in his chair.

"Tamsin waits until everyone is listening before speaking. He says, 'My champions, as you know, I have gathered you together to rescue my beloved consort, Lesser Wyrm Sythern, from the wicked mercenaries. They have captured my beloved, and are even now holding them as a captive in their dastardly lair. Great Wyrm Thalen has trusted us with this task and has promised a handsome reward to whoever reunites them with their child. I will not lie, this will be an arduous task. The road before us is long and littered with peril. We set out tomorrow at dawn. Rest well, my champions!' Tamsin wraps up the speech. So, you all had the chance to select your gear before the session, but tonight you can explore the citadel and make any last-minute adjustments." I say.

"Zelphod clasps a fist to his chest in salute," Errol says.

"If that's all, Maximus is going to the gardens. He stalks from the room, leaving the gathering behind in a huff," Max says. At least he's trying. Sort of. Good enough. I nod.

"Pebbles and I are going to spend the evening celebrating our leavetaking with the other dragon singers," Laura says.

"I've heard of the citadel's famed hot springs. Perhaps I could beg a tour of the grounds?" Gui asks.

"Our order has much to offer, I could show you around and we could get acquainted as we are to be companions?" Jude offers self-consciously.

"I'll take you up on that," Gui says.

"Guess that just leaves me and the prince," Errol observes, then in his Zelphod voice he adds, "How are you holding up, Highness?"

"I fear for my consort's safety. The mercenaries who took him are known for their cruelty. They have only given us a fortnight to meet their ransom demands," I say for Tamsin. The prince's stoic facade fades now that he and Zelphod are alone.

"We will save Sythern; I swear on my honor," Errol vows. "Now, we must prepare for our journey. Elder Yaren has provided our supplies, but I want to be sure everything is in order for an early departure."

After that, Errol gets a call that our pizza order has arrived. That's my cue to take each player off to do a private mini session while the others goof around and eat.

CHAPTER 5

Jude

The pizza place Errol chose offers a whole wheat crust, so I let myself indulge alongside the others. It's still not the healthiest choice in the world, but a couple slices of whole wheat veggie pizza won't throw off my usual diet too much. No one comments when I test and inject my insulin at the break room table.

I let myself get drawn into chatter about work and the game. Theo takes each of the others into the conference room to play out what their characters do the night before we leave on our epic quest. It's fun, but I sort of wish I could hang out with Theo more. Max chats me up a bit, since he's also new to the studio.

"Have you been out much? Seems like there's a decent nightlife but no one's interested in much more than hooking up," Max complains. "Like don't get me wrong, I'm not looking for forever, but it's been rough trying to make friends outside work, you know?"

"Have you considered that hook up hotspots aren't where you ought to look for friends?" Errol suggests as he grabs a slice of pizza.

"Worked out just fine with you," Max shoots back. "I got a sweet new job and a new friend out of approaching you."

"I didn't sleep with you, and we have common interests other than partying. Besides, I was only at that party because a friend in the industry was the organizer," Errol says.

Max scowls. "What are you suggesting then? Should I join a knitting circle?"

Errol shrugs. "Well, sure. If you enjoy knitting, then that's exactly what you should do. Or if you like tabletop games you could join a VentureQuest campaign with your supervisor and newest friend," he winks at Max, who gives him a sheepish look.

"Yeah, thanks for the invite, boss."

"I'm sure you'll get the hang of it. You're doing better than me, I'm clueless," I say, reaching out to pat Max's arm, the same way I'd nudge Gui if something upset him.

"Maybe. I don't think Theo likes me much, though," Max says.

"He'll get over it, if you put in the effort. We aren't a super battle focused group," Errol says.

"And now he's glowering at me," Max grumbles. He shrugs away from my hand on his shoulder and juts his chin toward the conference room. Sure enough, Theo is scowling toward the three of us.

"Max, your turn," Theo barks it like a command. He turns on his heel and retreats into the conference room. Laura returns to the group as Max stuffs his last bite of crust into his mouth and obeys Theo's summons.

Gui looks up from his phone, unglued from the screen at last. Paz must be ready for bed if they're done texting.

"Having fun?" Gui asks me.

"Sure," I say. I'm simultaneously glad that my character went off with Gui's and anxious about it. On the one hand, I won't be all alone with Theo for my not quite solo session. I'll be able to play off Gui's lead. However, Gui isn't stupid, and he knows me. Knows both Theo and I well. Will he be able to parse the tension between us? Or is it all in my head?

The tension must be just me. I'm the only one with a hopeless crush here. It'll be fine. I can hide being flustered over Theo paying attention to me. Plaster over any hint of my infatuation with nerves over doing this game stuff right. It will be fine. I hope.

One glance at Theo when he invites Gui and me into the conference room blows that hope out of the water, though. This is going to be hard. He's so animated as we play. Lit up like a kid at Christmas. Him letting me play in his game means something. Not anything sexual or romantic, but there's an intimacy to being invited into his inner world tonight. A bond forming between us as I give my brother's character a tour of the dragon citadel and try to get into character with him encouraging me along.

I get the sense this is something Theo only shares with friends, not lovers. Everything Gui's said about Theo tells me I can't be both. Theo doesn't do relationships, so I need to be okay with being his friend. If only my traitorous heart can get past this infatuation that wants to make him mine on a deeper level.

CHAPTER 6

06

Theo

Mini sessions with each player always pose a challenge. I run the risk that the other players will get bored or lose interest, and I have to balance that with giving each player a meaningful experience. I enjoy doing it this way to let everyone take the first session to get into character before we dive into their adventure. Pizza works to distract my other players from any boredom as they go through their last night at the citadel by turns.

I suspect my Max issue will resolve itself. Dude is not into the roleplay. He just wants to beat shit up. That is *so* not my style as a GM. I love an epic battle as much as the next guy, but there is so much more to the game than beating up monsters and maximizing damage.

If I'm lucky, he'll decide to find another gaming group and I can run game with Gui, Laura, Errol, and Jude. Then I can give Maximus Powers a gruesome death, which will motivate the other players and take out my dislike of the sorcerer. Or, if Max bails, I can play Maximus as a recurring villain. The backstory Max and I came up with—okay, mostly I came up with it and Max just nodded along—has fun potential.

I'm so caught up in planning for our next session as regards Max's life choices, that I barely notice the group departing. Tonight's game ended with the cliffhanger of everyone hearing the citadel guards sounding an alarm. That had always been my plan. But Max attacking the garden guardians to get at the rare fire phlox growing at its heart added a layer of intrigue. That development made me glad I'd taken each player or in Gui and Jude's case, pair of players, aside to do their RP in private.

"You like him," Gui accuses me when it's just us left to lock up and set the alarm code. He jostles my arm and I'm not sure if it's our usual friendly fooling around or if he's upset that I have a thing for his brother. Is this macho posturing BS to assert some sort of dominance?

At least he waited to confront me alone. Jude got swept away with the others when they left. I wasn't paying much attention, but I'd noticed Max's arm going around Jude's shoulders and Errol offering them both RP tips. The familiarity between Jude and Max still has me scowling.

I shove Gui away. He leans down to grab his backpack, like he hasn't just shattered any illusions I harbored of being subtle about my crush on his brother. I finish jamming my game stuff—pencils, rule books, laptop, dice, and notes—into my bag. Then I put my arms through the straps and scramble for the exit, as though I can outrun this inevitable conversation.

"Admit it, you do," he taunts again as we're leaving.

In an industry where overtime is the norm, we all have the alarm codes for if we leave after hours. I use the excuse of punching it in to avoid eye contact as I splutter, "What? Who? Shut up."

"Jude. You like him," Gui states it like an indisputable fact.

"I..." don't have a response. Jude is cute. I enjoyed playing with him tonight. Once he warmed up to the roleplay, he dove into it and that made him even cuter in my eyes. But that shouldn't matter, since I don't date.

"He's into you," Gui throws that little tidbit out, as though it matters. There's wariness in his tone. A tacit acknowledgement that this can't end well.

"Okay," I say flatly, pretending not to care.

"I've never seen you crush on anyone before," Gui continues. Apparently, I missed the memo where he appointed himself as my fairy godmother.

"That's ridiculous." I wave away his outlandish claims. "And you would look terrible in fairy wings and a frilly tutu, also, glitter. Everywhere. And you would deserve it," I add for good measure. Gui as my fairy godmother is not a terrible style on him, but I'm not about to boost his ego by telling him that. And I'm pretty sure fairy dust is like glitter on crack; that shit gets everywhere. Gui wisely ignores most of what I said, knowing my habit of going off on tangents. He takes the comment in stride, holding the door open for me to exit onto the street. The sidewalks are wet from rain, but it's currently more of a light mist than even a drizzle so we don't bother with umbrellas.

"Noted, Theo. You know he's been living with me for over a month now, and tonight is the happiest he's been since he started work," Gui continues, undeterred. "Let him down easy, okay?"

I shrug, self-conscious. It's pointless to lie to Gui. He's known me for close to ten years. Ever since I was a lowly intern in the US working my first job as a generalist and he was a junior animator fresh out of school. We'd both worked for a small studio producing commercials back in the day. It had been the first job each of us landed in the industry and we'd bonded.

Gui had worked on some big movies in VFX and I'd done a stint in television before making my way to video games and narrowing my focus to lighting.

Gui and I stayed in touch from those early days and took up a full-fledged friendship when we found ourselves as co-workers again five years ago, here at Eye-On. He is, hands down, my best friend, and he knows me too well for me to get away with bullshitting him.

"Right. Message received; you want me to keep my hands off your brother," I reply, bitterness tinging my words.

"No. I mean, yes, but I just don't want either of you hurt. If you're into him for more than a quick fuck, then that's different," Gui says.

"I'm not. Relationships give me hives." I play up a fake shudder.

Gui rolls his eyes. "All I'm saying is, Jude's a total romantic. If you can give him your heart, then that's great."

My stomach lurches at the thought of letting anyone into my life for more than sex. Not happening. Not even for cute as hell Jude.

"I won't deny he's a hottie, but hearts and flowers are not my jam. His heart is safely off limits, okay? I promise not to hurt your brother." I say. Our eyes meet and Gui looks more sad than satisfied by my promise. His expression softens, like he wants to push me toward changing my stance. Not happening. I deflect the conversation into safer territory, "Jude is a perfect addition to the group, I think he'll fit right in with you all. Max, not so much."

"Think Max will be back?" Gui lets me get away with the blatant subject change. He gives me a resigned glance that says I haven't heard the last of this, but that's an issue for future Theo.

"Hard to say. I'll give him a few more sessions to adjust his attitude before I lower the boot hammer." I decide.

"Can you even do that IRL?" Gui asks.

"I'm the GM, I can do whatever I want," I say with airy bravado.

Gui laughs. "Sure, man, whatever you want, until the players rebel and depose you from your throne."

"Pretty sure if you try, you won't get to find out what happens with Sythern and Tamsin," I threaten.

"And what makes you think we care?" Gui asks, hiding a hint of a smile.

"You wound me!" I clutch at my chest, miming a grievous injury, even staggering a few steps along the sidewalk. Gui grabs my arm to steady me before I fall off the curb and into traffic. He rolls his eyes at my antics.

"Don't get hit by a car, or you'll really get wounded. But for real, if Max keeps misbehaving, we'll back you in asking him to move along, okay?" Gui lets go of my arm now that I'm done being dramatic.

"Thanks. I'll pull him aside for a chat before the next session, I sort of have an idea," I say. It's a vague and unconventional idea, but Errol told me he invited Max to play because the guy is having a hard time adjusting to living in the city. Max is fam in the sense that he's queer like the rest of us. As much as I'm annoyed by his play style and his touching Jude, I don't want to just kick him out of the group. Not unless he leaves me no other choice.

"We got your back, dude." Gui bumps our shoulders together in solidarity.

"Thanks, man," I say as we reach the stoplight across from The Taphouse, a bar where Eye-On has employee discount cards as one of our perks. Some days, I love my job.

We wait for the light to change while watching the passing traffic in silence.

It's Friday night, a couple beers and a shared appetizer at The Taphouse sound perfect before I hit the bars on Davie Street. Or Grindr might yield a cute guy to flirt with and get Jude out of my head. He's Gui's brother, and it's a small world. I don't want to deal with an ex in the industry when things inevitably fall apart. Let alone forcing Gui to choose between me and his brother if a fling turns messy.

"Earth to Theo," Gui grabs my arm to get my attention, the light has changed.

"Oh, sorry, man. Just thinking," I say as we hustle across the intersection.

"About Jude?" Gui suggests with faux innocence. I know he's only goading me, but it still gets under my skin.

"No! Of course not," I splutter.

Gui gives me a knowing smile. "Really? My bad, what were you thinking about?"

"That I need to get laid. I might hit one of the hook up joints on Davie, after this."

My packer du jour is reliable at passing a grab test. I can pull a drunk dude looking for a bathroom blowjob without having to deal with disclosure. That, plus my hand, will have to tide me over. I don't feel like talking tonight, I just want an anonymous orgasm to take the edge off my attraction to the soft-spoken Jude.

CHAPTER 7

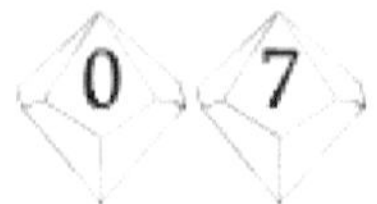

Jude

This lingering crush is worse than I'd feared. After our game, I can't shake that Theo is exactly how I remembered him from our night together. Loud, outgoing and flirty. He is also really freaking hot when he gets all fired up about running his game.

I'd give a hell of a lot to have a guy light up about me the way he looked when he described the backstory for the campaign we're starting. The way he smiled, just for me, when I tried to get into character made me trip over my words, my heart stuttering with nerves. Stupid, traitorous heart still hasn't gotten the memo that nothing more than friendship is happening between us.

I want to hang around Theo and Gui to keep chatting after our game ends, but that's a terrible idea. Instead, I tag along with Laura, Errol, and Max when they leave.

"You're both joining us?" Errol confirms with Theo and Gui before we go.

"Yep," Theo agrees absently. "I have time to grab a beer or two before ditching you lot for my other plans."

My heart sinks as I consider the sort of plans he might have for this late on a Friday. Plans that involve sex with someone who isn't me. Damn it, I swore I wouldn't go there with him again.

"See you there." Gui waves us away.

"Cool, I'll grab a table big enough for all of us," Errol says.

Max loops an arm around me and leads me out of the darkened studio. It's strange being at work after hours like this. Everyone assures me I'll get very used to overtime in this industry, and I don't doubt it. I've already stayed to work late a few times. Tonight is the first time I'm among the last people leaving the building, though. It feels different without the buzz of people working on the rows of quiescent computer stations.

"So, what did you think?" Errol asks as the door to the stairwell closes between us and Theo.

"Eh," Max says as we all make our way down the stairs. "I'll reserve judgment. You're right that he gets into the RP."

"Hey, there's nothing wrong with enjoying the role-play part of role-playing games," Laura comes to Theo's defense before I can work up the guts to say anything. I like Laura and Errol, but I don't know them well, and this is the first time I've interacted with Max much.

"I warned you about that," Errol says with a shrug.

"You did. I'll give it another few sessions and see how it goes. I'm used to more emphasis on combat, but it's cool that Theo puts so much effort into the storyline." Max shrugs. We're quiet as we file out of the building and onto the sidewalk. It's raining, only a light shower, but steady enough that I join the others in digging my umbrella out of my backpack.

"What did you think, Jude?" Laura nudges me once we're all situated and headed toward the bar.

"I've never played before, but I liked it," I admit.

"Aw, it will thrill Theo that he got to pop your gaming cherry." Laura elbows me in the ribs with a chuckle. My cheeks burn as I flash back to the other time he popped my cherry. I'd had sex before, anal and otherwise, but always bottoming. Fucking Theo was… nope, I don't need to be thinking about Theo nearly naked and writhing on my dick. I've been jerking off to that memory for months. I never thought a guy in just his underwear could be hotter than if he was totally naked, but yeah, I'm super into it now.

Errol snorts. "That'll go straight to his head. You had fun?"

"Yeah," I reply.

"Are you planning to keep coming, then?" Laura presses. Geez, I hope I'm hiding how much I want to come with Theo again.

"Yeah," I choke out and then I cough on air. Can I get any more awkward?

Errol pats my back. "Almost there, they have a huge rotating list of local craft beers on draft. You like beer, Jude?"

"Yeah," I agree, it still seems weird that I'm of age here with none of the fanfare of reaching a birthday milestone. The closest thing I've had to that was Theo insisting on taking me out to ring in the new year. And look how well that ended. I'm hung up on him, and he's doubtless slept with a dozen other guys since our hookup. Worse still, I know I was a fumbling mess, so I doubt he'd want a repeat, even if he was so inclined. No matter how incredible that night seems in my memories.

"Hello? Jude?" Laura waves her hand in front of my face to get my attention, and I blink back to reality. The rain has mostly tapered off and I'm the only one who still has my umbrella held high, the others have theirs folded up, ready to enter the bar.

"Sorry, what?" I ask.

"We're betting on what the alarms at the citadel going off meant," Errol informs me. He holds the door to The Taphouse open for all of us and we deal with our wet umbrellas, leaving them by the crowded stand near the door. Laura tugs me right up to the bar.

"Oh. I thought it was because Maximus snuck into the restricted part of the gardens," I say. Not that I know what Max did in the gardens, but it seems reasonable to assume it wasn't above board.

"Well, sure. We're discussing if there was a bigger attack as well. And whether it might mean we don't get our supplies from the citadel before we go after the mercs," Laura fills me in on the conversation I missed with my woolgathering.

"Oh. That would suck. I'm supposed to get that nifty amulet that lets me appear human for an hour. You know, to blend in if we have to go through human lands," I say. At least, that's what I'd discussed on the messaging app with Theo when he helped me make my character. That had been an exercise in self-denial, chatting with him and keeping it strictly about the game. My heart had leapt right up into my throat with giddy anticipation when I saw his name pop up on the intra-office messenger. And then dropped right back down to somewhere around my toes when I realized he was going to continue pretending like there was nothing between us. Well. Not pretending; there isn't anything between us. That's my entire problem. I ought to find someone more attainable to get hung up on.

We order our beers, mine an alcohol free light beer. I *can* drink alcohol, but most of the time it's not worth dealing with the effects on my sugar the next day. Laura orders for Errol and herself. She gets wings and cheese fries for the table too. If I spend more time with Gui's buddies, I ought to bring my own snacks. None of their choices fit with my usual carefully balanced diet.

We take our drinks to a corner table Errol has somehow claimed, despite the seating area being packed with people in various stages of inebriation. The others chat about our game and work. Max keeps trying to draw me into the conversation. He reaches out to touch my arm or nudges me with his elbow every chance he gets. I keep defaulting back to staring at the door like a lovestruck idiot waiting for my crush to arrive.

When I drop the thread of conversation for the third time in a row, Max and Errol exchange loaded glances. Laura leans in close to whisper to me, "Hey, you don't have to be nervous around us. We want to be your friends, independent of your brother, you know?"

"Huh? Oh, right, sorry. I guess I just get shy in crowds," I fib. At least they think I'm waiting for Gui and not Theo. The only thing more mortifying than an unrequited crush on the guy because he gave me a drunken pity fuck would be everyone knowing about it.

I'm saved from further comment when Theo and Gui arrive, laughing and joking. They rock paper scissors in the entryway. Theo smashes Gui's scissors, then gives him a shove toward the bar, calling out his order loud enough that I can hear him across the room. Then Theo comes to our table, leaving my brother to grab his drink.

The way he grins when our eyes meet stirs up every emotion I've been desperately trying to suppress. I gulp my beer and hope I can keep my emotions off my face until I can make my excuses to head home.

CHAPTER 8

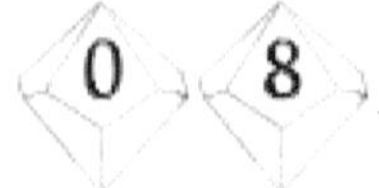

Theo

Jude licks his lips and the way he's staring at me as I approach the table makes me think he might rather lick me. God, I absolutely cannot go there again. If Gui told me that Jude had all but accepted a job at Eye-On with us, I never would have let things progress as far as they did between us. Sure, he'd hinted, but still.

Somehow, I'd figured if Jude was back in Cali after our one wild night, it would be easy for both of us to move on like it never happened. Out of sight, out of mind. Well, so much for avoidance. Now, he's very much in my sights and on my mind. Has been for weeks, for all my efforts to dodge him, and by extension, Gui.

It's one thing to flirt with my best friend's innocent baby brother. Getting just drunk enough to make poor choices with him, and then letting him fuck me after he admitted I was his first, bypassed stupid and leapt right into catastrophic. I know better. Since that night,

I've tried to do right by him. Avoid leading him on at all. I have his number, I could have called or texted or just checked how he was doing and his progress with the move. Instead, I settled for getting my Jude updates through Gui.

My reasoning is that the only thing worse than ghosting Jude after sex is getting his hopes up for something I can't give him. I know myself too well to think I can knock off the flirting entirely. I'm turning into a giant fucking ball of mixed signals with Jude. So better to leave him alone.

Too bad I can't seem to remember that resolution as I smile at Jude. I wedge myself in to stand between him and Max at the table. The move forces Max to slide down a seat, because I've apparently developed an even bigger masochistic streak and want to torture myself with the unobtainable.

"Hey, Jude," I sing the opening line of the song to him, teasing and light. And since I'm me, my friends will let me get away with over-the-top displays. So I belt it out, serenading Jude in front of our friends in the middle of a bar like something out of a ridiculous rom-com.

Jude rolls his eyes and ducks his head at being made the center of attention. Max snorts and takes a sip of his beer. His dislike for my GM style must not be personal if he's gonna laugh at my jokes. Or maybe he's just laughing at me. I opt to give him the benefit of the doubt and offer him a grudging smile.

"I'm sure that's the first time he's gotten that, Theo," Errol reaches across the table to shove me.

"Sorry, couldn't resist," I say. Not in the least because Jude makes me want to sing. There's this lightness in my chest when I get to spend time with him. The same stupid fluttery sensation in my gut that I know from experience is a lie, but I can't seem to shake the crush.

"It's fine," Jude rushes to assure me. "My mom loved that song. It's not the most original thing I've heard, but that's why she chose my name. She used to sing it to me."

Great, I reminded him of his dead mother. Fuck, now I feel like an ass for teasing him with it. "I'm sorry," I repeat, truly meaning it now. I don't want to hurt Jude. That's the last thing I want, which is why I should stick to my earlier resolve to leave him the heck alone.

Jude puts his hand on mine and squeezes. I like that far too much, I should pull away. He's so sincere it hurts when he says, "No, don't be sorry. It's nice. Reminds me of her. In a good way."

Before I can say anything to that, Gui appears with our beers.

"Hey, scoot over, Theo," Gui shoves in between his brother and me. I don't miss the warning glower he shoots my way. Can't blame him when I just agreed not to toy with Jude's affections. I don't complain, just move down one seat, forcing Max to move again, and take my beer, swallowing half of it to help me keep my big mouth shut.

A server brings over a platter with a round of shots and our usual appetizer order. I snag a couple of wings and down my shot. My phone buzzes in my pocket with a message notification. I glance down and see a guy I've messaged a few times says he's en route to a bar. If I'm still interested, maybe we can hook up, no pressure. I tap out a quick reply that I might see him there. It's a five-minute bus ride from here and he's got a longer commute, so I shoot the shit with the gang for another half hour before I take my leave.

I've got a potential lay on the hook. If I'd rather sit around trying not to flirt with Jude than get laid, well, that's all the more reason I should leave. Do not pass go, do not collect two hundred dollars. Epic failure on the forbidden temptation check, but I'm not going there again. Not when I know Gui would kick my ass for leading Jude on, no matter how rah-rah he sounded about us dating. He'll get pissed if I fuck Jude and run, and that's all I can promise. I toss down money for my share of the tab and say my goodbyes.

"Hate to take this party on the road, but I've got a date," I waggle my eyebrows at my friends.

"Go on then, we see how it is," Gui complains. He tosses a napkin at me, but there's an underlying resignation to the teasing that's different from our usual banter. "Go get laid instead of hanging out with your friends."

"Uh huh, says the guy who's holed himself up in his love lair with the new boyfriend for the past four months," I fire back. For good measure, I lob his napkin grenade right back at him.

Errol snorts and hides a smile behind his beer.

"Have fun," Laura says in a knowing tone. Because, yeah, she knows me well enough to realize that 'date' is almost always a euphemism for hooking up when it comes to my love life.

I glance at Jude; fuck, I'm a bastard for liking the disappointment in Jude's eyes when I stand to leave. I ruffle his hair, unable to resist that last touch. Then I walk out without a backward glance. I pull out my phone on the bus and message the guy to let him know I'm bailing. I can lie to myself and say that I overdid it drinking with my buddies, but the truth is, I don't want to sleep with someone else. Not when all I can think about is Jude's big brown eyes and his guileless innocence when he was railing me on New Year's Eve. Fuck my life.

CHAPTER 9

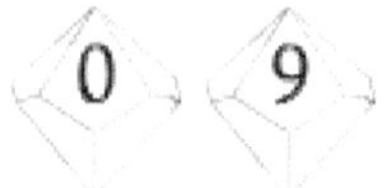

Jude

The next week of work follows the pattern set by the first several. Every shot I'm assigned seems make or break as I get used to the studio, and I work late most nights to make sure I hit my quotas. Gui tells me I shouldn't devalue my time. I can see his point. I'm not getting paid for the unapproved overtime, but I take too long to get my shots just right if I don't put in the extra hours. Once I get used to how everything works at a bigger studio, I'm sure I'll adjust to the faster pace required here. Hard to believe it's already been a month since I started.

Anyway, it's not like I'm the only one working late. I'm not even the only one on my team to linger after hours. Besides, I don't mind it much. Sticking around late means I don't have to listen to my brother and his boyfriend fuck before Paz has to go to bed on worknights. I'm careful not to stay out too late, so I don't disturb him. But late enough to give them alone time.

It also doesn't hurt that working long hours means I have less time to obsess over Theo. He was definitely flirting with me before he ran off to meet his date the other night.

Date. Right. I saw the app he was using before he left. While I prefer relationships to casual sex, even *I* realize that a Grindr date you meet after midnight is a hookup, not a date. I have zero right to jealousy over Theo. He isn't my boyfriend. He's just a friend I slept with once. It shouldn't hurt that he would rather sleep with a stranger than hang out with me.

So I'm not jealous or hurt. I've considered downloading one of those apps I saw on Theo's phone the other night at least a thousand times. Except I doubt I'll find the epic romance I want on a hook up app. Or at the clubs Theo pointed out to me on Davie Street. Or at the bathhouse Gui mentioned visiting downtown when he was single.

I'm also not going to meet the love of my life by spending every spare moment shackled to my work desk. If only figuring out where *to* meet Mr. Right proved as simple as determining where *not* to meet him. I'm sure if I tell Gui that I'm angsting about finding the love of my life, he'll tell me I'm way too young to worry about chasing after romance. I sigh and glance at the clock.

Shit, I need to wrap up what I'm doing or I'll be late meeting my friends. Paz doesn't have work tomorrow. When Gui mentioned that fact to Theo, he declared we were all going out together for once and leveled a death-glare at Gui until he agreed. Paz invited his cousin, Alice, and her girlfriend along. We're getting dinner together to kick off the evening. Errol, Laura, and Max are walking over with us. I'm even supposed to meet the famous Pia, the person Max and I got added to the group to fill in for. Their partners have baby duty so they can get out of the house alone for a few hours.

I wrap up my work and pop over to our group chat on the intra-office messenger. Theo has been spamming the channel with messages about tonight all day. The latest one is a GIF about 'getting this party started'. It's six now, and a new message appears.

Theo: Time to get our weekend on. I'm coming up there to get you people. Geez, bunch of workaholics, the lot of you.

Gui: Slacker. No wonder they keep you locked in the basement. You're a party monster.

Errol: I just got out of a meeting, I'll be ready in five.

Laura: Ugh. I am sick of this stupid fuzzy-ass owl. Whose goddamn brilliant idea was adding in an extra playable character at the last possible moment? *Battle Fox* doesn't need an avian PC. It's bullshit. We don't have the time or the budget to develop a fucking feather sim that even compares to the detail on the mammal fur we developed. It's going to look like shitty-ass crap unless production can magically dig a bigger budget out of their out-of-touch asses. We need another month of dev at the fucking bare-assed minimum to make this work.

Max: Tell us how you really feel, Laura. Don't hold back.

Laura: It's a cook ducking @$&#! and duck production, too!

Errol: Should I consider that an official request for a deadline extension, Laura?

Laura: And double-duck autocorrect for throwing more nonconsensual birds in my face when I'm already having a feather-fueled breakdown! /rant

Laura: Sure, Errol, if it will get me out of modeling each individual feather for the next eternity, you can print that out and just redact the expletives.

Max: So, you don't actually want to fuck production then? Or buy us all pet ducks? Maybe cook us a duck dinner?

Laura replies with a photo of herself smiling sweetly as she flips Max a double bird. She's captioned the image: 'these are the only birds I have for you'.

Laura: That's me saying, as kindly as possible, go off and fuck yourself, Max. I'm done. Meet you guys on the second floor in five.

I should say something, even just to confirm I'm coming too. Or that I'm excited to go out with them. I type a few words, delete them, start again, then realize everyone else has already logged out. I sigh, shut down my workstation, and grab my coat and bag.

Gui waves me over to his desk, Max is already standing there, chatting with him about something. As I join them, Theo's raised voice proceeds him out of the stairwell. He's got Laura and Errol in tow. Theo dyed his hair neon violet this week. I like the vibrant color on him. He wore a matching purple onesie to work today for some donation thing the studio does to raise money for different charities on the first Friday of the month. His pajama has a unicorn head hoodie, and he's expounding on why nightclubs should have more theme nights and how costumes shouldn't just be for Halloween and cons.

"We get it, Theo," Errol cuts into his tirade about costumes. "You like being the loudest person in the room, even when you've got your mouth shut."

Theo guffaws at that. The rest of us laugh too. "Maybe I do," Theo admits wryly. "But so what?"

"So nothing. Are you wearing your pajamas to dinner or changing before we go?" Errol asks.

Theo crosses his arms over his chest, "What's wrong with what I'm wearing?"

"Nothing." Gui slings an arm around Theo, giving him a gentle shake. "Wear whatever makes you happy, Theo."

"You make a very fetching unicorn," Laura adds. I agree with her and I'm jealous that she's comfortable enough with him to grab his hood and pull it up over his head. Theo laughs and adjusts the hood so it doesn't obscure his sight.

"Hey, ask before you rub my horn, Laura," he teases.

Max rolls his eyes, but he says, "You do you, man."

"Why, yes, I do plenty of men," Theo purposely mishears him, "thanks for asking."

"I didn't ask," Max assures him.

"Children!" Errol interrupts before they can argue more. "Aren't we meeting Pia and Paz for dinner?"

"Paz booked the reservation for seven, we're fine," Gui says. "We should head out though, if everyone's ready?"

We all agree that we are, and the friendly banter continues around me as we walk. At one point, Theo drops his arm around my shoulders.

"You're being quiet, Jude. How are you adjusting to the

studio?"

"I like it. Other than stressing over quotas. I think I'm getting the hang of things," I reply, leaning into his arm around me. I can almost pretend it's more than a friendly gesture. Except Theo is touchy with everyone. He was just tickling Errol before he dropped back to walk with me.

"Glad you're getting used to it. On our internship together, Gui and I shared many a round of beer commiserating over how demanding studios can get. It's all a matter of balancing time versus quality, right?" Theo asks.

"Yeah," I agree, "I'm having to let go of wanting every little detail to be perfect so I can get stuff in on time."

"You'll get there," Theo encourages me. "The more you do it, the faster you'll get and your quality will improve, too."

"So, practice makes perfect?" I quip. My traitorous mind goes right to other things I could practice with Theo. I want to do *him* again. Get better at that. Good enough that he might consider giving me more of himself than one night in his bed that we never talk about again.

"You got it," Theo winks at me. Gui calls his name and Theo removes his arm from around my shoulders fast enough you'd think my touch burned him. He jogs ahead to talk with my brother. The half-pitying glance Gui shoots me for a fraction of a second after Theo joins him makes me wonder if he just wanted to separate us. But that's probably a paranoid thought. It's not like Theo feels the same way I do. If he is meddling, Gui just wants to protect me from getting too attached.

Paz and his cousin are already seated when we arrive at the restaurant. They wave us over to a table in the back. I sit wedged between Gui and Theo. None of our friends bat an eye when I pull out my meter and calculate how much insulin I need with my dinner. It's nice not to have to explain myself. Pia arrives a little late. They appear frazzled. She greets the table and flags down our server to order a cocktail.

"I am officially hanging up the parenting hat until morning!" they declare. "Rain is Emil and Gregor's problem tonight. I love that little booger to death, but Renny needs a break."

"Here, here!" Theo says.

"That kid couldn't ask for better parents than you three," Laura adds with a fond smile.

Theo says, "Now, it's been ages since you had a drink with us; we've got your tab covered for the night, right folks?" He shoots a look around the table, but everyone is nodding.

"Right," we all agree.

"Aw, thanks, Thee." Pia leans in and kisses his cheek with a noisy smack of their lips on his skin. I take a large swig of my water to shove down my envious reaction to the casual affection. "Now, tell me about all the April first shenanigans I missed yesterday," she demands. The others comply, eager to retell their favorite stories. I kept my head down with the pranks flying all around so I don't have much to contribute to the conversation.

After the food, Theo and Pia lead us on a bar hopping tour down West 4th Street. From there, we hop a bus across the Burrard Street Bridge to a club just off Davie. I order soda water with sugar-free mixers because I'm just not up for a lot of booze tonight.

We all hit the dance floor together. Pia gets wasted within a few hours. She sticks around to dance a while longer, grinding with Theo, Laura, and Errol. Gui and Paz are in their own little world together. Alice and her girlfriend have been bickering all night, so I avoid them and end up pairing off with Max to dance at the edges of our group.

A pretty twink approaches Theo at some point, tugging on his unicorn outfit's tail and flirting. Theo breaks away from our group to make out with the new guy in a corner booth. At that point, Laura and Errol leave to take Pia home. Errol has a car, and he hasn't had nearly as much to drink as the rest of our group. Just a beer with dinner.

The last I saw of Gui and Paz, they were sucking face while they did their best to fuck with their clothes on in the middle of the dance floor. I can't find Alice and her girlfriend. That leaves me dancing alone with Max again, and trying not to shoot longing looks toward Theo and his twink of the day.

"Want to try making him as jealous as you're acting?" Max suggests, his mouth near enough to my ear to make me shiver.

"Huh?" I ask.

"Theo," Max clarifies. "You haven't been able to tear your eyes off him all night."

I turn in his arms, looping my wrists around his neck as we move to the beat. "I can tear my eyes away from him," I say. He's right that I don't want to, though.

"You could try telling him how you feel," Max suggests.

"There's no point. Theo doesn't do relationships," I say.

"Huh, is that so?" Max's hands slide from my hips to my ass. I tense, but he doesn't pull me against his body or grope me or anything, just rests his hands on my ass as we dance. Max tips my face up toward him and asks, "You sure about that? Because he's watching us right now. He looks just as happy about my hands on your ass as you looked when he had his tongue down that Jude look-alike's throat."

"He didn't look like me," I protest.

"Sure, Jude. My bad, he just had the same height, build, eyes and hair, not like you at all. Fifty bucks says if I kiss you, Theo will swoop in and steal you away."

"You're about to owe me fifty bucks," I say, and then I yank his mouth down onto mine. Max's mouth is soft and warm against my lips. His breath is boozy. His tongue sweeps over mine, tasting of rum and soda. He gives my ass cheek a gentle squeeze. Then a heavy hand lands on my shoulder and Max is smirking against my lips.

"Hey, Jude," Theo's voice carries over the music, "mind if I cut in?"

"I was just about to call it a night," Max says. He leans in close and hisses near my ear, "told you so."

Theo glares after Max's retreating form until I tap his shoulder.

"You wanted to dance?" I ask, holding up a hand in invitation. Theo takes it and tugs me close to his body. The song changes to something slower and we sway together as the singer croons about love.

"What happened to that guy you were flirting with?" I ask, trying not to sound bitter about it.

"Who? Tony? He wanted to leave," Theo replies with practised nonchalance. I'm not surprised, considering how hot and heavy they were getting.

"And you didn't go with him?" I ask.

Theo looks uncomfortable. "I saw someone I'd rather dance with."

"You'd rather dance with me than fuck Tony?"

"I'd rather do a lot of things with you than Tony, sure," Theo remarks.

I huff out an exasperated breath. "What are we doing?"

Theo chuckles and looks pointedly toward our feet. "We're dancing, obviously."

"You know what I mean," I grumble, tugging free of his hands.

"I don't know, Jude. I really don't. If you would rather go back to kissing Max, I'll back off." Theo steps away, running a hand through his hair. It's hard to hear over the music, so I keep my reply succinct.

"You're an idiot," I say.

"Thanks?" Theo looks hurt.

"I only kissed him because he bet me you'd ditch Tony if we did," I step back into his arms and speak close to his ear.

"How much did I lose you?" Theo asks, a smile in his voice.

"Don't worry about it," I brush him off.

Theo searches my face. Whatever he sees there must convince him to drop the subject. The song changes to something more uptempo and I let Theo pull me against his body. We dance until I'm sweaty and horny and his lips are on my neck making me crave more of his touch.

By mutual agreement, we slip off the crowded dance floor. Theo leads me out the back door into an alley. He pushes me up against the brick wall and kisses me hard. We aren't the only club patrons out here, but the others ignore us and I'm too wrapped up in Theo to care who sees us. He kisses me until I'm breathless. His hand delving into my pants and gripping my dick.

"Want to suck you while I jerk off," he says, voice

husky with desire.

"Here?" I ask. Theo nods. His mouth on my neck sends tingles of pleasure all along my body. "Yeah, okay," I agree.

Theo crouches in front of me, he grips my hips to steady himself, then gets my dick out and teases the head with his tongue. I moan and rut into his hand.

"Hold still, babe," Theo instructs. I'm pretty sure he just uses that endearment during sex to avoid the awkward moment of forgetting someone's name or using the wrong one. I wish he'd call me Jude. Not that he's calling me anything, with his mouth full of my cock. I stuff my fist in my mouth to keep from crying out as heat engulfs my entire length and Theo swallows around me.

He's moaning around my dick and the vibrations are enough to make my toes curl. Theo's head bobs along my length. I rest a hand in his vibrant hair, eliciting another of his throaty moans. I remember how much he liked his hair pulled last time and I give an experimental yank. Theo groans and I can see how fast his hand is moving inside his pants.

I tug harder and Theo pulls off my dick long enough to say, "Oh, fuck, yes, babe, make me take it." Then he dives back down on my dick and I grip two fistfuls of his hair and fuck his face. The gagging sounds he makes have my dick throbbing with need, but I pause, making sure I haven't taken the game too far. Theo pats my thigh in encouragement when I stop. So I thrust down his throat, loving every minute of his body yielding to mine. Loving the way he's getting off on pleasuring me. The intense pleasure of fucking him as he takes every inch of my dick down that hot, tight throat of his.

I don't last long after that. Theo grips my ass hard to

keep me from pulling out too soon. He's still touching himself, the movement less urgent now. Like he's playing with himself after coming and he's too sensitive for anything more intense than a light brush of his fingers. I tug on his hair to encourage him back to his feet. Theo stands and leans against me, sharing a salty-bitter kiss with me.

"Thanks," I say, though the word is wholly inadequate for how good he made the experience, the filthy alley only adding to the illicit sense of getting away with something.

"Don't mention it." He swipes a hand over his lips. "Want to go back inside?"

I don't. I want to stay here with him leaning against me and bask in his warmth.

Instead, I say, "What about you?"

"I'm good, I got off on having you throat-fucking me. I like it on the rough side like that," he explains. His unself-consciousness over the declaration makes me envious.

"You sure? I can suck you back at your place, if you'd be more comfortable with that?" I suggest.

"Aw, are you angling to spend the night again, Jude?" Theo teases. His hand cups my cheek, and he looks at me like he wants to kiss me. Not the hot and heavy lust-fueled kind either. The emotion in his eyes is tender. Sweet, even.

I flush, I hadn't intended to invite myself back to his place, but I'd be lying if I denied wanting it. "Only if you want me to."

For a second I'm sure he's going to say that me in his bed again is exactly what he wants. Then his expression closes, and he frowns, pulling away from me. "That's a bad idea, babe. Come on, we should find your brother and make sure he and the others get home safe."

Theo steps away, straightens out his clothes, and slips back into the club with me trailing behind him. I wish I could say I'm surprised by the sudden distance, but I expected it.

CHAPTER 10

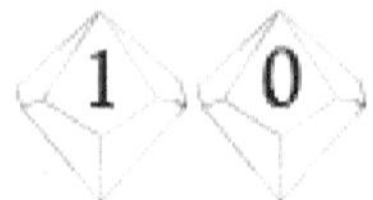

Jude

Another week passes and I'm getting more confident in my work. I've found a groove, squeezing in a jog or a swim at the Y before work most days. This week, I only stayed late one night to finish up something I was in the middle of doing. I'm only still at the studio after five tonight, because we have our next game.

My intra-office messages are flashing with a new message, but that's been their perpetual state since Gui added me to the game group chat before my first session playing. Gui's buddie constantly message each other throughout the workday. Some messages are about the game. Laura and Errol had an entire conversation about how she can take better advantage of her dragon companion. Theo interjected every so often to remind them of the rule modifications Laura and he agreed to when they made the character.

Earlier, Theo invited Max to a private chat to discuss something, and now Max is sending vague messages about a surprise at tonight's session. Gui sent me a link to some dice he thinks I'd like, since I'm borrowing his spare set for now. The shiny rainbow-hued set is pretty, but I'm not sure if I want to invest in dice when I can't seem to get my mind off Theo.

I'm not sure how healthy feeding this crush will be for me if I keep playing with them. Then again, Gui's gaming group are the only people I've hung out with other than Paz and his cousin. It's harder to make friends here than it was back home. Or maybe it's just not as easy without school as a natural common ground to start from.

The newest message in the chat is from Gui asking if I'm *still* working and wondering if I want him to grab me anything from the cafe. He's headed there before the game to meet Paz and grab snacks. Everyone else wanted caffeine. I shoot back a reply saying I'm not hungry.

I like the cookies Paz makes, but they're hell on my glucose and I'd rather not fuck my diet anymore than going out drinking after our game will do. Speaking of my sugar, I grab one of the protein bars I've got stashed in my desk so I can keep my levels from dropping when I'm working late. I test my sugar and inject before the snack and wrap up what I'm working on as I eat it. I finish posing the character in the shot I'm blocking out, save the file, and log off my workstation for the night.

When I get to the conference room, Theo is sitting alone. He's setting up his laptop when I walk into the room. Theo glances up at me. His smile freezes on his lips when he sees it's me.

"Oh, hey, Jude," Theo says with false cheer.

"Hey," I reply awkwardly.

"Excited to play?" Theo asks.

"Yeah. I think so. Um," I glance back to make sure the others aren't about to walk in on us. There's no sign of them yet. know Gui can't be back from Sin and Chocolate so soon. If I want to clear the air with Theo, this is the best chance I'm going to get. "Can we talk for a second?"

"That's what we're doing, right?" Theo says, he rearranges his dice and papers to avoid looking at me.

"Look, I get that you aren't interested in a repeat, okay? Can we not be awkward? It's not like we can avoid each other without Gui getting suspicious. I'd like to be friends with you. It will make both our lives easier if we can just forget what happened on New Year's Eve and at the club. Pretend it never happened, right?"

"If that's what you want," Theo agrees. He sounds relieved, but there's regret in his eyes when they meet mine.

"It is," I insist. That bald lie doesn't come close to convincing my heart, but I'll get over it. I set my bag down and claim the chair closest to Theo. I can be around him without obsessing. Just watch me.

"Okay. Friends." Theo nods. "Just friends. How are you liking the game?"

"It's fun. I felt kind of silly at first, but it helps that everyone gets into character."

"Yeah. That's my favorite part."

"I couldn't tell." I knock our shoulders together, teasing him is friendly, not flirty, right?

Theo gives a self-conscious chuckle. "Yeah, well, when I was a kid figuring myself out, RP was the first place I could explore my identity, you know? It was safer to explore being a guy in a game than just jumping into asking the kids at school to call me Theo and change my pronouns."

Well, so much for keeping things light. That is personal shit, and it makes me feel for him in ways I shouldn't if I want to get over my crush.

"Oh." I scramble for a response and settle for prying into his personal life even more. Not my brightest move, if I want to get over him. "Gui says you come from a small town up north. How did everyone handle your coming out?"

Theo shrugs. "Could have been worse. There were a few assholes, but my family and the school administration were supportive. People talked. Small town gossip meant everyone and their mother knew about the first out trans kid at the high school, but nothing terrible happened to me. Overall, people were supportive or indifferent. I think my mom suspected something before I had the words to tell her I'm trans, since I'd been cosplaying as guys at cons for years by then. She drove my nerdy ass to the city while I was playing a boy enough times to realize how much happier I was in that role, you know?"

"I'm glad you had people who accepted you," I say, touching his hand. Damn it, this is not a conversation between casual friends, but I can't seem to help myself. "I got bullied," I blurt. "For being gay. At my school, before my parents sent me to live with Gui's family."

"I thought they adopted you after your folks died," Theo says, looking taken aback.

"Yeah, they did. But I already lived with them." I swallow hard. "I was born in Cali, but Dad got a job in Nashville when I was ten. The kids at my school there were relentless. They decided I was gay before I even realized it about myself. I begged my parents not to make me go every morning for most of the year. It didn't help that I was still figuring out my insulin regimen, and testing, and how to give myself shots. That was the year I got diagnosed. Anyway, Gui's dad works for a private school, so he pulled strings to get me in there at a reduced tuition. My parents decided that I'd be happier back in California. I was living with Aunt Mere and Tio Carlo so I could start school while my folks were figuring out the job situation with moving again so soon. They died before that happened."

"How did they die?" Theo asks. "I mean, only answer if it's not too hard to talk about it."

I've answered that question so many times it's gotten easier to say the words, less raw. "Carbon Monoxide poisoning, from the downstairs neighbor's garage. Their rental didn't have a detector. They were in bed. The authorities told us they just never woke up. I think they'd have chosen to go together like that. If they got a choice."

"I'm sorry, Jude." Theo knocks his knee against mine under the table. His words sound so earnest they hurt. I get the sense he means so much more than he's saying. I shrug, but the way he watches me warms me right down to my toes.

"Thanks."

"I'm sure they wouldn't have left you, if they got a choice," Theo adds.

"Yeah," I say, unsure where to take the conversation. Our eyes lock and I lean toward him. Is it wishfulness or is he leaning in, too? Is he experiencing the same magnetic pull toward me that seems like it's tugging me toward him?

We're saved from an epically stupid move by Laura, Errol, and Max joining us. All three of them have takeout containers and they're chatting animatedly as they enter the room. Theo straightens away from me and makes grabby hands at Laura. "Did you get my burger?" he demands.

"I said I would, here," Laura pulls the paper-wrapped sandwich out of her bag and hands it over to Theo. He grins and unwraps his prize, biting into it with a low moan that does nothing for my renewed resolve to view him as nothing more than a friend.

While the others take their seats and dig into their food, I focus on my phone. I could join them, but I've settled into a schedule after all the disruptions of moving. If I want to drink with them later, I'm better off not fucking with my food and testing schedule more than that. I've been eating a snack, like the protein bar, around now and then having dinner at home around nine. I've got leftover whole wheat vegan pizza from my lunch in the fridge in the kitchen. That ought to tide me over and counteract the effects from the after game drinks I intend to consume.

"Aren't you eating?" Theo asks me between bites of his burger.

"Um, not hungry, I'll eat in a bit, if that's not a problem?" I reply.

"Not at all," Theo agrees. He returns to his food. Not long afterward, Gui arrives with sweets and a tray of coffees. I never acquired the taste for it, and since caffeine can fuck with my sugars, that's just as well. The kitchen in the break room has herbal teas. I like the idea of something cozy to sip on while they're all eating, so I excuse myself to make a cup.

Gui catches me as I'm leaving, "You doing alright?"

"Yeah, fine. Need to grab a drink."

"Sounds good, we'll wait to start until you're back," Gui claps me on the back as a pass him on my way to the break room.

CHAPTER 11

Theo

"Are you all ready to embark on your quest then?" I ask the group once they've made their final plans to leave the dragon citadel. They agree. Finally. They got hung up investigating the alarm from the end of the last session. A messenger from the mercenaries who took Sythern caused the dragon guards stationed in the citadel gardens to sound the alarm, as far as anyone at the citadel knows.

After devouring their dinners, the entire debacle of getting the party to depart took absolute ages. First, they went around questioning everyone and looking for answers that they utterly failed to find.

Max watched smugly as they all tried to figure out what's happening with his character. If any of them had a perception stat worth shit, they might have realized magic played a role in the attack in the garden. The messenger was no magic wielder. They might have noticed the trampled area in the center of the gardens, or the freshly harvested fire phlox plant those dead guards were out there to protect. Instead, they fumbled around for the better part of two hours investigating at the citadel for any evidence Maximus was as sketchy as they all suspected before admitting defeat, then gearing up for the road.

There was a break thrown in, when Jude had to reheat his dinner and do his testing thing. But now we can finally delve into what I actually planned for tonight's session.

"The dragon singers and the monks gather to send you off from the citadel with their well-wishes. The road away from the citadel curves into a canyon out of their sight."

"I ride ahead to scout the area. You can never be too careful," Gui says, speaking as Carl the ranger.

"I observe the rocks, looking for danger," Errol adds, meaning he wants to roll a perception check. I hit the button on the RNG and play up a wince.

"Zelphod sees a rocky canyon," I say.

"Yep, those rocks sure are rocky," Errol quips.

"I check out the area up close," Gui says.

I press the button again and snort. "My, oh my, the canyon has rocky rocks and crevassey crevasses," I tease.

Gui groans. "Are we about to get ambushed?"

"I have a bad feeling about the canyon," Errol grumbles.

"Too bad we don't have our sorcerer to cast a protective spell on the party," Laura comments pointedly toward Max. All of them want to know why Maximus Powers disappeared overnight. Right after the human mercenaries who took Prince Sythern sent a messenger with a fresh ransom request. No one has a clue why the messenger killed two monks in the gardens as he made his escape.

Max looks amused at their fumbling. Poor Jude seems overwhelmed with all the roleplay. His valiant efforts to play along make me all mushy with feelings. Errol is getting frustrated with his character's limitations and the fact Laura has cantrips she keeps forgetting to use. Gui and Laura seem into the mystery of it all, so I don't move things along right away.

"Too bad," I agree with false sympathy and a conspiratorial smile for Max. He grins back at me, knowing what's coming since I discussed it with him earlier. Laura scans her character sheet so I give her a minute to figure out what she's doing. "If only there was a bard around," I prompt when she still seems to struggle with picking her next move.

"I sing a song of strength," Laura hastens to announce. "Also, this is the reason I suck at support classes, I always forget which spells and abilities I have and how long they last."

"No comment on your aptitude. Song of strength gives allies in the listening range +1d3 buff to strength for the next five rounds of combat or an hour out of combat," Errol explains.

"Yeah, I have that noted," Laura says.

"Roll for it," I say. Laura gets a three for maximum benefit and pumps her fist in triumph, knowing my house rules, she hums a few bars of row your boat. Errol snorts. Gui chuckles and offers her a fist bump over her song choice.

"Theo likes to make us sing for real, hence I never play a bard class with him," Errol explains for Max and Jude's benefit. "Song choice is up for interpretation."

"What? Do you deny rowing builds arm strength?" Laura says defensively.

"Fair enough," I agree with her logic. "Okay, everyone in the party listens to Larris's song and feels stronger, as though a magical force has invigorated their muscles. You all have a temporary +3 to your strength."

"So, does that mean we hit harder?" Jude asks.

"It means you get three bonus points on strength based tests, including combat checks," Errol explains.

"Okay, cool, thanks Larris, I feel more prepared to face what's next," Jude says.

"Do you continue along the road?" I prompt when no one else seems to have anything to say.

"I do," Gui agrees. The others nod their agreement.

"So, you all step into the shadows of the canyon." I pause, giving them a chance to object. No one does. I roll a die for dramatic effect. Then I announce, "Once you are all inside the canyon, a loud bang followed by the rumble of falling rocks sounds from behind you. An enormous boulder now blocks the road back to the citadel. Out of nowhere, a figure emerges onto the pathway ahead of you."

"What kind of figure?" Errol demands.

"It is I, Maximus Powers," Max announces his arrival with an evil cackle. And okay, if I'd known letting him play the role of recurring villain for the campaign would get him into the RP, I'd have suggested it from the start. "Dragons will never again deny and humiliate me. Now that I have the fire phlox, no dragon will ever dismiss me again. But first I will defeat you champions of dragonkind and prevent you from installing yet another dragon in leadership!"

"Wait, Maximus? How could you betray us like this!"

Gui exclaims.

"Roll for initiative, bitches," Max crows. Okay, well I can forgive breaking character a little, I mean he's right, they need to roll.

We figure out the turn order for battle and then they go at it. Larris has the first action, with another song to buff the party. Gui and Jude attack. Gui rolls like shit, missing entirely. Jude rolls a natural twenty to everyone's delight, only to get confused when the attack whiffs right through the illusion spell Max had cast.

The party is failing perception checks left, right, and center today. Not that they know it. I roll those behind the scenes for them so they aren't all sitting there knowing that they got a one. Keeps them on their toes.

"What?" Jude asks, looking around the table like he's missed something, "but I hit him!"

"He's a wily sorcerer," Errol comments. "Must be an illusion spell."

I glare at him.

Errol sighs and holds up a die in question. "Knowledge arcana?"

"Go ahead," I agree, though I'd prefer if he tried to make it seem more in character.

He rolls, winces at the results and says, "he's a magic user, perhaps it's some sort of spell making our attacks fail."

I chuckle, because we both know I don't need to tell him he failed that check spectacularly. At least Errol memorizing all the rules means he isn't fighting with me over stupid shit.

"Alright, Zelphod is up," I prompt. Errol considers his character sheet. He examines both sides for some hidden ability that might help him here. There isn't one. He's not playing some fancy class with levels poured into specializations and hoarded magical artifacts. This time, he is just a run-of-the-mill level five fighter.

Errol sighs, flips his character sheet back over and reluctantly declares, "I attack Maximus, saying, 'you will pay for your betrayal, fiend!'"

Errol rolls a hit, barely, and his sword disrupts the illusion.

It's Max's turn now, he should have had the advantage, after setting up this ambush, but rolling a one will put a crimp in anyone's plans. "I cast a deep sleep on them."

"Roll," I say. Unless he fails badly, the spell's area of effect will knock out everyone except Larris and Pebbles. That will allow Max to make good his escape to return and taunt the party another day. He rolls well enough, and the party goes down. I narrate the spell and its effects, noting that Larris actually passes a perception check for the first time all night. She notices Max riding off into the distance on a stolen horse before she tries to rouse the party with another song. The attempt fails, so she just sits there watching them once she checks they aren't dead or in need of first aid.

It's early enough that we *can* keep playing, I have plenty more planned for tonight, but they took ages leaving the citadel and it's almost ten. If we keep going now, the next natural stopping point might have us playing until well past midnight. Not that I'd mind that, but I offer them the option. "Okay. Do we continue, or to be continued?"

"This seems like a natural stopping place," Gui says as he checks his phone.

"You just want to go home to Paz," I whine.

"And?" Gui shrugs. "If you had a sexy boyfriend waiting at home for you…" he trails off. I flip him off because everyone here knows I don't date.

Jude groans. "Well, on that note, I'm up for post-game drinks."

Gui pulls a face at him and Jude sticks out his tongue. I tear my eyes away with an effort.

"No can do," Errol says, pushing back from the table. "It's just as well we're wrapping up a little early, I have commissions I need to get done this weekend."

I nod in acknowledgment. Errol does amazing coal drawings when he isn't busy bossing other artists around at work.

Laura yawns. "I should turn in too, I promised Pia and co that I'd babysit Rain tomorrow so they can all get out of the house and have adult time. Ever since Emil and Gregor have been back at work, Pia's been struggling with feeling isolated."

"Max?" Jude asks, and I notice the hint of desperation in his voice now that it looks like we're all going home. If all of us call it a night, he'll end up stuck as his brother's third wheel. I mean, I could have told the guy that moving in with the lovey-dovey new couple was a terrible idea, but that was why humans invented noise canceling headphones.

"Sorry, can't tonight, I'm trying to cut back on my expenses," Max says apologetically.

Well great, that means I'm fucked either way. Or not fucked. I won't abandon Jude when I don't have a good reason not to join him after our game. But being alone and drunk with him again won't lead to smart choices for either of us. I sigh.

"I can buy the first round," I say. Max perks up at the offer. I know Jude has been paying for Max's lunches all week, but presumably that was about the bet Jude mentioned. Come to that, I suspect with the move and everything, Jude's short on cash too.

"That's cool of you, thanks, Theo. I guess I can come out for a beer." Max grins at me. Jude doesn't seem to know whether to act relieved or annoyed. A buffer between us should be a relief. I fucked up earlier with the emotional talk and letting him think there was any hope for a deeper connection between us. Gui told me that the kid is a hopeless romantic. I should have taken that warning more seriously.

"Great! Let's head out," I say. I gather up my stuff to put it all away.

"I just need to test before we head out," Jude excuses himself to deal with his medical stuff.

"Watch out for him, Theo?" Gui asks once Jude leaves the room.

"Of course," I agree with a flippant wave of my hand.

"I mean it, alcohol fucks with his sugars," Gui reminds me. As though he didn't read me the riot act when I sent Jude home hungover on New Year's Day.

Gui's sort of right. If I'd known how sick overindulging could make Jude, I wouldn't have encouraged him to drink so many shots. He'd been aware enough to ask for sugar-free mixers, though. Proof the guy can take care of himself and knows how to manage his diabetes without big brother's meddling. The tension between Gui and me is palpable, and the others hasten to clear out. We glare at each other as they say their goodbyes.

"I'll meet you guys downstairs, I have to grab something from my desk," Max lies. I'm pretty sure it's an excuse not to get caught up between Gui and I.

"Yep, heading out now," Laura adds. "Have a wonderful

weekend."

"Enjoy the baby snuggles," I say. "Send pics of Rain to the group chat, Pia hasn't been updating us enough."

"I'll ask if they're cool with more baby pics," Laura agrees.

"I'll walk you to your bus stop," Errol offers. "Catch you all later."

That leaves Gui and I alone.

"Your brother is an adult who has been managing his own damn sugar since he was a kid. He can go out drinking without a fucking keeper," I snap at Gui to break the awkward silence.

"He shouldn't, though," Gui argues. "It's not always easy for him to tell if he's drunk or low. Someone needs to check in with him the next morning to be sure he eats and takes his insulin."

"You saying I should invite him home and feed him breakfast?" I taunt. I shouldn't. Gui glares at me.

"No, you ass, I'm saying I don't want you to hurt him. Do you still expect me to believe that sleeping is all you did when he visited over the holidays?" Gui demands. He gets right in my face and whispers the accusatory words in an angry hiss. Probably because he doesn't want to risk Jude overhearing us arguing about him. Because it's ridiculous and this is none of Gui's business.

"I don't owe you a play-by-play. Jude is an adult," I say the last part slowly, emphasizing each word to drive home my point. For good measure, I poke my best friend in the chest.

Gui scowls, crossing his arms. He isn't ready to relent, though. "He's an adult who I care about, Theo. You know I love you, and I don't care if you fuck half the population of Canada."

"But?" I challenge him when he stops talking. "Am I not good enough for him, Gui?" I'm an idiot for asking. Of course I'm not boyfriend material. My longest adult 'relationship' lasted two weeks, and that was only because we couldn't figure out a sooner date for our second hookup between our busy work schedules. I prefer it that way. Casual is better. Simpler.

"I never said that," Gui snaps back. Then he sighs, resigned, as he drops his face into his hands. "Jude has a big heart, Theo. He believes in epic romance and getting swept off his feet by his own prince fucking charming. If you can't give him that, I get it. But don't hurt him by making him think you can."

"I'm not trying to lead him on," I admit, the fight leaving me. If only I could be that guy.

Gui gives me a shrewd look. "You like him."

It's the same accusation from a few weeks ago. This time I shrug uncomfortably and turn back to stuffing my game stuff back into my bag. Macho posturing won't get us anywhere. Gui takes my cue. He picks up his dice and collects the set he leant to Jude.

"It doesn't matter." I brush him off. "You're right that I'm not good for him."

"I never said that either," Gui says, frowning.

I shrug. He didn't need to say it. It's the truth.

Gui gives me a pitying glance. "Look, Thee, I don't claim to know what's going on between you two. If anything. I just know he's been weird the past few months. It could be the stress from uprooting his life and moving and adjusting to the industry. Or maybe I'm expecting him to act like the kid I knew before I moved away from home when he's an adult now, but he's different. And I don't enjoy watching him bury himself in work and pretend like everything is fine."

"Duly noted," I say, dipping my head in acknowledgement. "I'll make sure he gets home safe tonight. He was fine having a couple beers with us after the last session."

"Yeah," Gui agrees. "I know he has a handle on managing his diabetes, that doesn't mean I don't worry about him. If you'd seen how fast he can get really sick, you'd get why."

"I'll hope to just take your word for that," I say. I don't want to think about Jude sick. Gui sidles closer and tugs me into a hug.

"I care about *both* of you, all I'm asking is that you don't hurt each other, okay?" Gui rocks me from side to side, and ruffles my hair. I pull away, but I can't help smiling at him.

"Dick," I accuse him as I try to fix my hair.

Gui laughs and clucks his tongue at me. "So vain."

"Don't be jealous of my style," I shoot back, pulling out my phone to make a bigger production of checking if I'm still presentable. I primp a little more and Gui shakes his head at me.

"Finish packing up, you peacock," he teases. I put away my phone and shoulder my bag. Gui grabs the stack of books I forgot off the floor and shoves them into my bag for me.

"Thanks," I smile at him. Jude walks in and looks between us.

"Did everyone else leave?"

"Max had to get something from his desk, so he's meeting us downstairs," I reply.

"Okay, cool, you ready?" Jude asks.

"Bring on the beer," I agree with a slightly forced smile.

CHAPTER 12

1 2

Jude

It's official. I'm hopeless. Max leaves after one beer. Theo tries to cajole him into sticking around and sharing the rest of the wings, but Max gives us a knowing look.

"It's been fun, I'm glad I stuck with the game, you're not a bad GM. But I'm not hanging around playing buffer between you two all night," Max declares.

"It's not like that," Theo protests, but it sounds weak and Max just rolls his eyes.

"Have a good night," he grins at us before he gathers up his stuff and leaves.

Theo won't quite meet my eyes. He watches the bar around us as I nurse my beer. It's not the full-bodied malty stuff I prefer, this is heavier on the hops. I nibble on our appetizer between sips, the celery garnish is nice and crunchy. We sit in uncomfortable silence for a while.

Theo finally says, "You didn't tell me drinking could

be dangerous for you."

I roll my eyes. "So you had a chat with Gui?"

"Yeah, he told me you could go into a coma or something."

I sip my beer again. "Sure, if I'm an idiot about it. I have a pretty good handle on my insulin needs. I take less when I'm drinking and I keep to my usual dietary schedule. It's fine."

"You should have told me, though," Theo insists.

"In January?" I ask. Of course he means New Year's Eve, when else could he mean?

"Yeah, what if something happened while you were sleeping? I wouldn't have had a clue what to do," Theo says. It's not the lecturing tone I'm used to from Gui. Theo sounds more worried than upset at me.

I want to tell him I don't owe him that. But he's sort of justified. It would have been shitty if he woke up to find me in medical distress without the first clue what was happening. I drank more than I strictly should have that night. "Yeah. I guess I should have. Sorry. It wasn't exactly the first thing on my mind."

Theo flashes me a half-hearted smile. "In your defense, sex with me can be pretty mind blowing."

I shove his shoulder. "My mind wasn't the only thing you blew."

"Yeah, I seem to recall you blew your load too," Theo teases.

"And yours?" I ask, then bite my lip, wishing I could take back the question.

"Yeah. It was fun, Jude," Theo says, then before I can do more than smile brightly at how that admission fills me with hope, Theo crushes it ruthlessly. "That doesn't mean I want a repeat."

"Okay," I say. I can take no for an answer. "So, no repeat. Just friends. Want to go dancing? I'm not ready to head home and I should stop at one beer tonight."

Theo swigs from his beer, holding up a finger to forestall answering. I wait him out, taking another measured sip of my drink. "Just dancing?" he asks.

"Yeah," I agree. Theo is going to be a part of my life, so I'll just have to crush out my stupid crush. Maybe watching him pick up a stranger will get it through my head that he isn't into me. "I can be your wingman or whatever."

"Alright, you're on," Theo agrees. We sit and chat about work and the game session while we polish off the chicken wings and I sip my beer. Theo doesn't rush me, so I take my time. We catch a bus to Granville and Davie, and then I follow Theo to the club. The bouncer barely glances at my shiny new BC driver's license compared to the scrutiny my US ID got me when I was just visiting.

Theo pulls me into the crowd and before I know it, I'm surrounded by moving bodies and a thumping bass line. Bright lights strobe, giving the crowd an ethereal quality. I dance without self-consciousness. I'm still not graceful, but it's good to move. The press of warm bodies energizes me. I lose track of Theo at some point, the moving crowd having separated us.

It's fine, though. My head is floaty from the beer. I indulge in the fantasy that the big muscled guy grinding against me might want me for more than a single passionate night, if that. The wild idea Theo pushing between us is more than him being over-protective of his best friend's baby brother kicks my stupid heart and my dick into overdrive. I ignore them both and torture myself by continuing to dance with Theo like we're nothing more than friends. Like I can touch him without wanting more. Like his warm, boozy breath on my cheek doesn't make me want to... I jerk back before my lips press against him and I realize I feel off. Drunk. More drunk than one beer ought to make me.

My head is swimming, and I stumble off the dance floor.

"Jude?" Theo sounds worried. I turn and shake my head at him. "You're scaring me, are you okay?"

"I just need a snack," I try to say. The words come out slurred. Theo helps me over to the coat check for my bag. When the attendant brings it, Theo rummages around for my stuff.

"Have too good of a time?" The attendant chuckles.

Theo glowers at him. "Butt out of it," he snaps. Then he finds the pouch where I keep my testing supplies and my glucagon.

"This?" Theo asks, offering me the latter. I shake my head.

"No, the candy," I mumble. He finds the roll of lifesavers and I snort at how apt that name is as I tear the paper and pop three of them into my mouth, then chew. I unwrap three more with shaky fingers and devour those too. Then I get out my meter to see how much I fucked up.

Theo is shielding me from anyone who might want to gawk at the scene I've made, stumbling and slurring. He helps me to a secluded spot near the door and hovers over me like a mother hen. I wait a minute for the sugar to hit my system, relieving most of my wooziness.

When I'm steady enough to prick myself without shaking, I test my levels. The number on the monitor comes back in my usual range. Good. Still, there's every chance I'll end up hypo again, if not right away then soon. I'd calculated my insulin dose for our snack and one beer. Sure, the dancing might have impacted things, but it rarely hits me that hard.

"What happened?" Theo asks when I put my supplies away and seem less drunk.

"Low sugar. I guess I miscalculated the carbs in the beer. It was just a regular lager, right?"

Theo winces. "I got you a light. Sorry, Jude. Last time you ordered a light beer, so I thought..."

I sigh. "Last time I was planning on having other stuff. If I'd wanted a light beer, I would have asked for one. That explains why it tasted so blah."

"I'm sorry," Theo says, sounding miserable.

"It's okay," I assure him. "It was an honest mistake. I just expected three times as many carbs as I got, I should go find something more substantial to eat so my levels don't crash again." It probably didn't help that I was dancing after taking too much insulin for the beer and snack.

"There's a poutine place around the corner on Granville that's open late. Perfect for soaking up booze after a night out," Theo suggests.

"Fries work," I agree. Fat, protein, and carbs should keep me from having too much of a drop while I sleep. Not a healthy habit, but it's not like I go out drinking and dancing often. The first time Gui told me about poutine it sounded gross, but he made me try it a few weeks ago and I liked the gooey cheese. "You don't have to come with me, if you'd rather stay and try to find someone you can take home."

Theo rolls his eyes and yanks me into a rough hug. "The only guy I am interested in taking home tonight is you," he says fiercely. God, how I wish that was true, but Theo backpedals, saying, "I mean, in the 'making sure you get there safe' sense. Not for sex."

"I get what you meant," I assure him. My heart might be confused, but even through the fog still invading my mind, I know he doesn't mean it like that. "It's fine. I can get myself home."

"There's no way in hell you are walking out of here alone after that," Theo insists. "Let's get some food in your stomach."

I can't argue with that, so I follow him to the poutine place. Theo loops his arm through mine when I'm still not steady on my feet as we walk. By the time we get our food, I've mostly recovered, but the shared meal should keep my sugar from dropping too much while I sleep.

CHAPTER 13

Theo

I am an absolute shit for putting Jude through that. The way he shook as we walked off the dance-floor gave me a better understanding of what Gui had meant about not seeing Jude sick. He'd looked completely wasted despite only sipping from one beer over an hour ago.

It also drove home *my* point, that Jude knew best how to take care of Jude. If I hadn't tried to, 'help him out,' by getting him something he didn't ask for, and just assuming I knew best, he'd be fine. Some color is returning to his face as we share an order of fries smothered in cheese, gravy, and bacon.

He lifts a fry and gestures with it as he tells me a story about his school buddies. I focus more on the way his face lights up as he talks than his words. That's not a good sign. I shake off the dreamy gaze and focus on the end of his story.

"So, anyway, long story short, the fire breathing geckos devoured my dog, and I ran off to business school never to art again," Jude says.

"Sorry, what?" I ask.

Jude huffs. "Nothing important. You don't have to babysit me if you'd rather go back to the club, I can get a bus from here that will drop me a block from home."

I wince, because it's after one in the morning, so no, he can't. The night bus technically still runs, but it only comes once or twice an hour now. There is no way I'm sending him off on his own to stumble across the Burrard Street Bridge in the dark.

"Come on," I say, standing and grabbing our trash, "you can crash at my place."

He hesitates.

"You don't want to wake Paz at this hour, right?" I cajole.

"Yeah, okay, fair point. I can sleep on your couch," he offers.

"The couch is shit and you've never even met my roommates. You can sleep in my bed, I think we've already proven it's big enough for two," I counter.

He stares at me for a long moment, and then he shakes his head. "I don't have the energy to argue with you."

"Good. It's settled then, you're coming home with me."

We leave the cozy little late night eatery and head toward my place. Once we get to Davie Street, I sling an arm around him as we walk. We aren't the only two guys touching in this part of town. There are even pride pennants hanging from the streetlights. As we turn off toward my street, I drop my arm.

"So, did you have a good time, even though I tried to

kill you with bad beer?" I quip.

Jude giggle-snorts. "Light beer is not only an abomination against tastebuds, it also kills," he jokes back. "But yeah, I had fun. Can we try the dancing part again sometime?" He gives me this hopeful look and denying him seems like kicking a puppy.

"Yeah, Jude, I'd like that," I agree.

"Cool," Jude replies. We walk in silence for a bit, then he says, "I'm sorry I'm cock-blocking you. Some wingman I turned out to be."

"Hey, I'm not complaining. Looks like I'm ending the night with a cute guy in my bed, so I've had worse wingmen."

Jude shoves me. "Why do you say shit like that?"

"Like what?" I ask.

"Like you think I'm cute. Or implying that you want me in your bed. Or the way you got between me and that big guy at the club when he got handsy."

"You *are* cute," I reply. "As to the rest? I look out for my friends."

"Am I *really* your friend?" Jude asks, eyes narrowing.

"Yes." I stop and grab him to make him face me, not caring that we're blocking the sidewalk. "You are."

"You sure I'm not just your friend's brother?" he demands with a scowl.

"No. I had fun tonight, Jude. You make me want things I haven't let myself want in a long time," I admit.

"Why not?" Jude softens as he asks it.

"Because," I evade the question. I don't talk about this with anyone.

"Because, why?" Jude presses. He steps closer and pats my cheek. It would be easy to close the distance and silence him with a kiss.

"It's complicated, okay?" I take his hand and squeeze, lowering it from my face.

"How complicated could it be? Either you want me, or you don't." Jude steps away, turning his back and stalking toward my place.

"I want you," I call after him. He pauses and I jog a couple steps to catch up with him.

"What's so complicated about that?" Jude asks when we're walking side by side again.

I run my hands through my hair and take a deep breath. "I told you how I used to cosplay a lot before I came out, right?"

"Yeah?" He side-eyes me, like he's confused by the segue. Jude makes me want to tell this story, he's easy to confide in. No one, not even Gui, knows that Craig is the reason I swore off relationships and feelings. We walk close, hands bumping together every so often, tempting me to grab hold of him. I ignore the temptation.

"Well, I had a gaming group back home as a kid, right? My three best friends and I got the game books at the comic shop in middle school, and I fell in love with gaming. It was my escape from reality. I know I had it pretty good. My family is great, even if they don't get my interests, they love me. I'm the baby, so I always had someone looking out for me, you know? But in character was the only place I was free to be myself until I figured out why I felt so wrong outside of our games."

"Okay. How does that play into you hating relationships?" Jude probes as I figure out how to say the next part.

"So, in my game group, it was me, Paul, Jacob, and Craig."

"Okay?"

I blow out a sigh. "Craig and I started dating. And like I said, it wasn't bad when I came out to the community. I never felt unsafe in my hometown. Scrutinized and occasionally judged, yeah, but never unsafe."

"You don't have to tell me anything you don't want to, Theo," Jude says when I pause too long to collect my thoughts. His pace slows.

I draw in a deep steadying breath and wave off his concern. "Yeah, well, I owe you an explanation for why I can't be what you deserve."

"Why do you think that?" Jude asks, he's watching me and I shrink in on myself under his assessing gaze.

"Because I'll inevitably hurt you. The same way I hurt Craig and you deserve better."

"You could just not hurt me," Jude suggests, face set in a sullen pout.

"Relationships are fucking hard, Jude," I snap, tugging on my hair in frustration.

"Why?" Jude asks.

"Because!" I snarl at him. He glares at me and I relent. "Fine. Describe our night together."

"Which one?" Jude fires back.

"New Year's Eve," I reply, exasperated at him for needing to clarify and myself for giving him cause to ask, since yeah, we technically had sex twice now. "Unless you remember a different night when I let you fuck me and then sleep over?"

Jude gets as flustered as I expect at that, but he does as I ask after a moment's thought. "Um, well, it was like you said. We got back to your place, and I fucked you."

"Details, Jude," I prompt him. There's no one close by to overhear us as we continue toward home.

"Fine." He runs a hand through his hair and stares at the

sidewalk as he mumbles the recap. "I wasn't sure what to do. You talked me through it. You kept your briefs on and it was hotter than anything I'd ever imagined, fucking you like that. The sounds you made when I pulled your hair. You were so hot and tight and the way you moved—I thought I was going to come so fast I'd embarrass myself and leave you disappointed. I'd never experienced anything like it. I wanted more."

"Yeah? What were you thinking about?" I coax him into describing more.

"Not coming. How bad I wanted to come. How sexy you were and how amazing it felt. And... why are you asking?" Jude is watching my face now, suspicious.

"You know what I was thinking?" I ask him, unable to keep the note of challenge out of my voice.

"What?" Jude asks, voice as soft as the tentative touch on my hand, and he twines our fingers together. He's so guileless. If he was anyone else, I wouldn't say this shit. I never talk about the bad days. Who would I tell? Gui is my best friend and we talk about sex, but I only share the good details with him. I drove Craig away with all the garbage in my head and I don't want to lose anyone else the same way. I glance around to be sure no one is close by, cognizant that I talk too loud and Jude isn't as brazen about his sex life as me.

"When you were fucking me, I was thinking about how I'm never going to experience half of what you just described. I was thinking about the fact that I was so—envious isn't quite the word, but close enough—of what's between your legs, I didn't even want to look at, let alone touch, what's between mine. Dysphoria hit me hard, it's just this sense of wrongness? I left my underwear on so I wouldn't have to take off my packer. I asked you to pull my hair because I needed the pain to distract me from my thoughts. It's easy to hide shit from another guy for a night or two. But relationships mean communication. It means talking about that shit and being open and I..." I shake my head, unable to force out the next part.

"You what?" Jude prompts me.

"The last time I shared this shit with someone, it was too much for him to handle," I say.

"How so?"

"We fought." I shrug, like it's that simple. "It was stupid. I told him I..." I trail off, swallowing hard and shaking my head. Unable to finish the admission.

"You what, Theo?" Jude asks, his tone soft.

"I told him I was thinking about killing myself," I blurt.

Jude's grip on my hand tightens until it hurts. "Do you still feel that way?" he asks, barely above a whisper.

"No. I have no desire to hurt myself. That isn't the point, Jude." I tug on my hand and Jude lets me go. "The point is, I told him how hard I was struggling. I told the boy who said he loved me how much it fucking hurt inside my head all the fucking time. And he told me I was a selfish bastard for thinking of doing that to him and my family. He was furious I'd said it. Demanded promises not to say it again. As though not saying it would somehow stop me from being depressed. We fought. I told him I never wanted to see him again." I draw in a shuddering breath.

"That's awful, Theo. I'm sorry," Jude says. It's clear how much he means it, too. He's so earnest.

"Yeah. It sucked. That night was probably the closest I ever came to actually acting on those thoughts. I loved him, we talked about everything. I came out to him before my family. He'd known every part of me since we were little kids, and my shit was too much for him to handle. The next day I came out to my mom. She kept me home from school and took me to Van to get new clothes and a new haircut."

"I think I like your mom," Jude says. "I'm sorry Craig hurt you."

"Mom will love you. All of them will." I shrug off his concern. "Everything with Craig was ages ago. And I hurt him too. I couldn't stop seeing him at school, but I cut contact with him. We didn't talk again for years. And I let our other friends believe he broke up with me over my being trans. I guess I thought it would be easier for him if people at school thought he hadn't known while we were together. That was bullshit, I get that now. But I was still figuring shit out. Anyway, our friends were protective of me, so they took my side and Craig didn't have any other close friends. It was shitty of me to make him as isolated as I'd felt when I couldn't be myself. Craig hurt me, so I lashed out and hurt him back. But that's the sort of shit that happens when you let emotions get all tangled. Things get complicated. Relationships just lead to people getting hurt," I conclude, since I know I'm rambling.

"And you're still afraid anyone you let in might hurt you the same way," Jude says.

"No. I'm not afraid it might happen, I *know* it *will* happen. You haven't been around when I'm not doing well. I don't want to be in my head sometimes, Jude. Why the hell would I subject someone else to me? Especially someone I care about."

"You might find someone who loves those parts as much as the rest of you? I know it's terrifying, Theo. You think I don't know how scary it is to take a leap? To not be sure of the landing? My first boyfriend dumped me because I got sick."

"What?" It's telling that I want to punch the teenage prick who hurt Jude. But then I never denied I liked him, I just know that it's a terrible idea to act on that attraction.

"When I get sick, like even just a cold, my sugars go all out of whack. I wasn't great at managing my levels back then. A stupid cold that would have posed a mild inconvenience to any of my classmates put me in the hospital. Diabetic Ketoacidosis, DKA. Gui was the one who found me unresponsive in my bed when I didn't come downstairs for dinner. If someone hadn't checked on me that night, the doctors said I could've just never woken up. I'm pretty sure it scarred Gui for life. For months after, he used to come check on me before he went to bed and when he woke up in the morning. Sometimes I'd open my eyes, and he'd be standing in my doorway staring at me while I slept."

"Like a creeper," I tease, because checking up on Jude is exactly the sort of overbearing, lovey sweet crap I can picture my bestie doing.

"Pretty much," Jude agrees, a smile tugging at his lips. "Anyway. When I got better and returned to classes, my ex couldn't cope with it. He basically told me he didn't want to end up with someone who had a chronic illness. It scared him. And I get it, I got scared too, thinking about the things that can happen if I don't manage my levels. No one wants to face their own mortality at fourteen, right? The thing is, not thinking about our problems doesn't make them disappear. So I got serious about managing my condition, and I realized that anyone who can't see past my diagnosis to the person I am isn't worth my time, anyway. And I think that's true for you too, even if your 'garbage', as you call it, is mostly in your head. That doesn't make it any less real than mine and it doesn't take away from who you are as a person anymore than diabetes makes me unlovable. If you ever felt that way again, if it hurts that bad, I'd want you to tell me. As your friend. Or whatever else we are. Even if it's just as your best friend's annoying little brother who has a hopeless crush on you."

"Not so hopeless," I mumble, squeezing his hand like the lifeline it is.

"Yeah?" he asks.

"I really like you, Jude. If anyone was worth trying to let in like that, it's you. But I'm not sure I have what it takes to open myself up to that kind of pain again."

"It doesn't have to hurt. We can figure out ways for you to get what you need without making it the focus. Like last time. You did what you needed to enjoy it, right?" He looks at me with those big pleading eyes and I pull him closer to my side, allowing myself the luxury of brushing my lips over his temple.

"Yeah, it was good," I confirm.

Jude flashes me a relieved grin, "Good. So, it's simple then. You just tell me what you need, and I'll do my best to give it to you. If you want to tell me what you're thinking or that you need something, I'll listen. Whatever you need to be comfortable with sex and experimenting with a relationship, we can figure it out together."

"I don't know if it can be that easy," I hedge, terrified that what he's saying makes sense.

"It works well enough with your one-night stands," Jude points out. "One way to be certain, right?" he insists.

God, he can be persistent. Not in a bad way. He respected the hell out of my need for space for months after our first night together. But I've been encouraging his interest, flirting with him every time we're together, and he meets me half-way every time. Maybe I can do this. Jude just proved he's willing to be as vulnerable with me as he's asking me to be with him.

"Okay." I relent. "We can see how it goes. Go out dancing and fool around and see if open, honest communication doesn't drive one of us to run for the hills."

"I'm not running anywhere, Theo." Jude gives me a knowing smile, then he swings our joined hands and pulls me up the path to my apartment. I'm not sure what to expect inside. Everyone else I've ever brought home, I would have fucked. Jude leaves his shoes by the door, then goes right to my room. He strips off his jeans, then sets them on top of his bag beside my bed. He tests his sugar again, mumbles that it's good enough, and crawls under the covers in his t-shirt and boxers. I slide in next to him, laying on my back to stare at the ceiling. Jude snuggles into my side.

"This is nice," he mumbles, his breath tickling my neck. "You okay with cuddles?"

"Yeah," I agree, patting his back awkwardly. I'm usually fucked out and mellow by the time my bed partners are just laying there with me, but this works too. His warm weight pressed against me is nice.

"Good night, Theo," he says sleepily.

"Good night, Jude," I reply. He drifts off to sleep and I pull out my phone to google diabetes and drinking and hypoglycemia so I know what to expect and reassure myself that he's fine.

CHAPTER 14

1 4

Jude

I wake up to my phone buzzing annoyingly somewhere on the floor and a leg thrown over my hips. Theo's neon purple hair is tickling my face and I smile as I smooth it out of my mouth and squirm free of his body and the blankets. Theo moans a protest, but he snuggles back into the bedding without waking, so I answer my phone in a low voice.

"I'm still alive, Gui," I assure him without waiting for him to greet me.

"Good," he says, shameless in his checking up on me. "Where are you?"

"At Theo's place. We were out late and I didn't want to wait for the night bus."

There's a long pause, then Gui asks, "Did you sleep with him?"

"We did nothing other than dance," I assure him, letting my exasperation color my voice. I don't need a lecture about my sex life. Theo is gun shy enough without Gui reading him the riot act like I'm some delicate flower who needs my honor defended. Besides, it's the truth. "Not that it's any of your business."

"You're right," Gui admits. "You know I worry because I care about you, right?"

"I know, bro. I can take care of myself, though. Anyway, I need to go grab breakfast and do my morning med thing. I might go for a walk before I head home, so don't send out the search party if I'm not around until later, okay?"

"Alright, I get it. I'll back off," Gui relents. "Love you."

"Love you," I say, a bit warmer than the rest of the conversation. Of course, that's when Theo sits up and gives me a wide-eyed look of horror, like a deer in the headlights. I gesture to the phone I'm holding to my ear and he gives me a sheepish relieved glance before pulling the sheets over his head. "See you in a few hours, Gui, bye," I hang up the phone and nudge the blanket lump next to me. "Relax, Theo, I'm not declaring my love to you. Gui called."

"I gathered that," Theo mumbles from under the blankets.

"Is your morning breath so hideous you're compelled to hide it? That's stuff I should know if we're going to be sleeping together." I prod him again.

Theo peeks out from under the blankets. "Are we going to be sleeping together?"

"I'd like to be, yeah," I reply. "I need to test my levels and do my morning dose, what do you have for breakfast stuff?"

Theo grimaces. "There might be some freezer burnt waffles, if my roomies haven't found them?"

I laugh. "Ok, well, we can go out then."

"There's a diner a few blocks down that does a mean hangover special," he suggests, running his fingers through his hair.

"Can we google the menu?"

"Yeah, sure," Theo grabs his phone and types in the name, then hands it to me with the menu pulled up. "So, do you like, need to plan out what you're eating for your insulin?"

"Yeah, basically. I calculate the dose based on my carbs and my current levels. Then I just dial the pen to the right dose and jab myself."

Theo shudders. "I hate needles."

"Don't you have to inject your T?"

"Nope." He grins and points to a pump bottle by his bedside table that I'd assumed was lotion. Or, knowing how much Theo fucks around, lube. "Topical gel, I just smear this on my shoulders every morning. You have no idea how excited I was when the doc told me I didn't need to inject. I mean, it took me a while to remember to apply it every day, but it's part of my routine now. On that note, you shouldn't touch my shoulders, cause it can transfer. Not that I think it would hurt you, or whatever. I have to be careful about keeping covered up when I hold Rain, though. Wouldn't want to hurt the little munchkin, you know?"

"Pia's baby?" I ask.

"Yeah. Shit, was that totally insensitive? Here I am whining about needles when—"

"You're fine," I hush him with a finger to his lips. "It's part of my life, I'm used to it. It's easier to view the injections as the tools I use to claim control of my health. It's why I prefer regular testing and injections over continuous glucose monitoring or an insulin pump. I like having direct control, and not feeling tethered to a device that's stuck into my body. No point dwelling on the negatives. At least my supplies are way more affordable here. Anyway, we should eat. Assuming you want to hang out with me today?"

"Yeah. I don't have any plans," Theo replies with the sort of bluster that makes me think he's downplaying how much he wants to spend the day with me. Or I could be projecting. "Glad the move has been good for your medical stuff. I've been jumping through hoops for over a year trying to get my phallo covered, but at least it will be covered, eventually. I doubt if I could even consider it if I lived in the US. Although, I guess a lot of insurance plans have to cover it now. With the new laws? I don't get how your USian system works."

"Yeah, I won't defend our healthcare system. My insulin and testing supplies are ridiculously expensive back home. Phallo's surgery for your dick?"

"Yeah, dick surgery," Theo smirks at me. "If you couldn't tell from my verbal diarrhea last night, the bottom dysphoria gets pretty bad for me sometimes. So, just waiting for the province to approve payment, since they only approve a few for payment a year. It's kind of pricey. Not that BC is brimming with trans guys looking to get surgery, but you know," he shrugs. "They actually do the procedure in Montreal. There's supposed to be a clinic opening here, but I've already started the process to go through Quebec, so switching would mean more waiting. Took a year just to get my first consultation and that was about a year ago, like I said. I could go private in the US, but money. Ugh, that reminds me, I need to make another appointment for electrolysis."

"Why?" I ask, curious how the two thoughts relate.

Theo gives me an assessing look, like he's not sure I truly want to know. I roll my eyes at him, and say, "You don't have to tell me."

"It's fine. For the procedure I want, they make the new dick from my forearm. And since I don't want a hairy dick, electrolysis kills the hair follicles. Got a dermatology consultation after my surgical consult last year. I've had several sessions already, but my electrologist wants me to come in for one more before the surgery. Just to be sure," Theo holds up his forearms, showing off the dark hairs on his right arm in contrast to the smooth skin on the left. "So, that's been a whole thing. It's frustrating, because I just want a freaking surgical date, but it's all a big waiting game. I was so psyched when I got my first consult, thinking it would happen soon, but no, I've got more hoops to jump through followed by more waiting."

"Oh, that stinks, I hope you get a date soon."

"Fingers crossed," Theo agrees. "They said I'd hear back by mid-April, last I checked with them, so it should be soon."

"Good," I smile, the conversation isn't as awkward as I'd have expected. Theo's trust in sharing this with me warms my heart. "So, um, speaking of genitals and stuff, you said you were okay using your front hole, is that still true?"

Theo shrugs. "Sometimes it's fine. I promise I'll let you know when it's not. They'll take it out during the surgery. I asked about having it done when I got my total hysterectomy last year. My surgeon says they prefer to do it with the urethral lengthening, so they can use the tissue."

I nudge my knee against his as I ask, "So, does that mean you don't want kids?"

"Not kids I carry anyway," Theo shudders. "Um, so, since the yeeterus of the uterus is complete, no worries about knocking me up. We should probably still use condoms, though. Easier cleanup with my prosthetic dicks, and I've had a fair few partners."

"Condoms are fine for now," I agree. I hope this is a conversation we can revisit later. I like the idea of being skin-to-skin inside him someday, but I'm not about to push him to make more of a commitment than he's ready for.

"Yeah, cool. Sounds good," Theo agrees with an emphatic nod that makes his hair flop into his eyes. He brushes it back.

"No problem," I assure him. Theo is too quiet. So I ask, "You thinking of running?"

He laughs and shoves me, "No. Thanks for listening. Come on. Let's eat before you pass out or something."

"I'm not just going to drop over with no warning, Theo," I explain before his smirk lets me know he was kidding. Good, because I manage my diabetes well. I've gotten in tune with my body since that DKA scare as a teen. I'm feeling pretty normal this morning. A little hungover from the hypo episode more than the beer, but fine overall. Theo excuses himself to the bathroom with an armful of clothes, and I pull out my testing supplies to check my morning sugar. A little low, nothing alarming. I drank last night, so I expected that.

Theo doesn't linger in the bathroom. He comes back shirtless, and it's a bit of a shock to realize this is the first time I've seen his bare chest. He catches me staring as he works his meds into his skin.

"Can I help you?" he asks, giving me a cheeky grin.

"How about giving me a closer look after breakfast?" I suggest, trying to match his flirty tone.

Theo grins. "Sounds like a plan. Breakfast, back here for orgasms, and then I wanted to swing by the Granville market to pick up bagels."

"I've been meaning to check out the market, you cool with me tagging along?" I ask, trying to sound casual.

"Duh, I wouldn't have mentioned it otherwise." Theo waves toward my disheveled clothing. "You want to borrow clean clothes? We're about the same size."

"If it's not a problem?" I ask.

"Help yourself." Theo gestures to his closet, and I grab a fresh shirt at random. I pull it on and Theo laughs. "Excellent choice," he comments.

I realize why when I glance down. A rainbow striped cartoon rooster is splashed across my chest with the caption 'I like cock'. It's totally him to be that bold about who he is. Theo the 'I don't give a shit what anyone thinks' fuckboy Gui has told me stories about for years is a far cry from the vulnerable guy who spilled his guts at my feet last night. Both are aspects of who he is.

"You can take a mulligan on your shirt choice," Theo offers.

"No, I like this one," I say, patting the rooster. "This way I can pet your pretty cock whenever I want," I tease.

Theo shakes his head at me, but he can't quite hold back his chuckle. "If you're sure. Pretty sure it's a shirt of 'detect enemies'."

"Nice." I grin at him. I'm not too worried about hostility in this part of town. We head out to the diner. I bring my bag along with all my stuff. My insulin pen makes it easy to dial up my dose at the table before we eat breakfast. It took me a while to get comfortable injecting in public. A few bad hypo episodes when I mistimed it or the food took too long to arrive cured me of any shyness.

Now I prioritize my health when it comes to my insulin and using it in public. Once our food arrives, I take my dose. I appreciate that Theo doesn't draw attention to it, just continues our conversation.

We chat about work and compare Gui stories. And that leads to how sappy he is with Paz. That devolves into chatting about exes. Well, my exes and Theo's many hookups. All the while we're stealing touches and swapping heated glances. He teases and flirts as easy as breathing, and it brings out the same energy in me. By the time we get back to his place after eating, I'm desperate to touch him.

He's on the same page because he drags me down the hall to his room, crowding me onto the bed to make room to shut the door. I like the way he muscles me underneath him and presses our mouths together. I open to him and his tongue fucks into my mouth as he grinds our groins together.

"What do you want?" Theo asks between kisses.

"Fuck me?" I ask. I've always sort of defaulted to being the bottom, and it's nice that he asks, but I want him inside me. Then I remember our chat about his dysphoria, and I add, "I mean, if using a prosthetic is something you're comfortable with."

Theo rolls off me and I grab for him, worried my request upset him. He gives me a tight smile over his shoulder. "I've got a few dicks I can use to fuck you, Jude, but they're in my closet."

"Oh, right."

"You have bottomed before, right?" he checks.

"Yeah." I nod. "Plenty."

"Okay then. You can use the washroom to clean up first. If you'd like. I've got stuff in a Shopper's bag under the sink." Theo gestures vaguely toward the bathroom.

"Okay," I agree. I slip out of his room and try to be quick about prepping myself in the bathroom that Theo shares with his four roommates. Thinking about them is a bit of a boner killer as I take care of stuff. I hear someone moving around in the hallway and I wait until it's silent again to exit the bathroom and return to Theo's room.

There's someone leaning against the wall, waiting with an armful of clean clothes when I open the door.

"Hey, I'm Theo's roommate, Jen," she introduces herself with a smile. "He must like you if you're still here for another round."

I'm not sure how to respond. It doesn't even surprise me she assumes any strange guy she finds in the hallway is someone Theo brought home for the night.

"Fuck off, Jen," Theo calls from his doorway. "Ignore her, Jude, Jen's just nosy."

I look between them as they bicker, super self-conscious that we're just supposed to go in his room to fuck when she's out here knowing what we're doing.

"It's not nosy if you're fucking on the couch, Theo," Jen shoots back.

"That only happened one time," Theo replies. "And you saw the guy. Can you blame me?"

"Can't fault your taste in men," Jen agrees, giving me a too keen once-over. "That guy had muscles for days. And you're not half-bad looking either, Jude, was it?"

"Yeah?" I say, uncertain. Not about my name, more about this blatant reminder that Theo doesn't do relationships. He told me why, but does he really want to change his lifestyle for me?

"Hey, imagine that," Jen snarks, not helping my sudden attack of nerves in the least. "He actually bothered to learn your name instead of just calling you 'babe'. You plan to keep this one around for once, Theo?"

"Again, and I say this with all the sincerity in the world, Jenny: fuck right off," Theo's bright cheerful tone is at odds with the words. He grabs my arm and pulls me into his room.

Jen laughs and calls after us, "Don't worry, Jude, Theo here generously gifted me with noise canceling headphones for Christmas so I won't hear a thing."

"Did you really?" I ask as I sink onto Theo's bed so he can shut the door.

He shrugs. "She wouldn't stop whining about how loud I get. Not just during sex either. Anyway, still want to fuck or did Jen kill the mood?"

"I could get back in the mood," I offer, reaching for his hand. Theo lets me tug him closer and we kiss. Gentle and sweet soon gives way to rough, possessive motions. Theo pushes me down onto the mattress and straddles my hips. As he grinds against me, I notice that he's hard in his pants.

"You're all ready to fuck me?" I tease, groping at his crotch.

Theo rolls his hips against me. "Ready when you are."

"Let me up so I can lose my pants," I squirm under him and Theo gives me a heated look. He leans over me, pinning my arms above my head.

"Make me," he challenges. We end up laughing as we wrestle for dominance. It's no hardship, grinding my hard on against him feels amazing. There's something thrilling about him holding me down. His gaze bores into me like he wants to devour me.

"You're not even trying," Theo accuses. I long since gave up the pretense of doing anything other than humping him.

Theo gets off of me and swats my ass. "Are you a greedy bottom, Jude?"

"I might be?" I reply.

"Strip and let's find out." Theo reaches for my pants to help me out of them without giving me a chance to obey. I let him undress me.

"God, you're bossy," I observe, amused.

"That a problem?" Theo asks, one eyebrow arched.

"Not for me," I say. Theo rearranges his clothing to get his dick out, it already has a condom rolled on. Theo slicks more lube onto his dick with one hand and along my ass with the other.

"Want me in here, baby?" Theo asks as he teases a finger around my rim.

"Yes," I agree. "Please." His teasing touches have me humping against his hand and he smirks at me in amusement.

"You gonna take every inch of me, babe?" he asks as he lines up his dick with my hole and presses. I don't miss the switch to impersonal pet names, and it irks me.

"That's the plan, *babe*," I throw the endearment back at him and he freezes.

"Sorry. You don't care for pet names?" Theo asks, all casual, but he pulls back from me so his dick isn't pressing against me anymore.

"You know it's not about the pet name," I say.

Theo settles back on his haunches and I regret calling him out on his intimacy issues when he was about to stick his dick in me. He lifts one hand to caress along my flank.

"You caught that, huh?" Theo sounds resigned.

"That you don't use my name when we're fucking?

And the only time you call me babe is when we're naked or naked-adjacent? Yeah, Theo, I caught that."

"I'm sorry, Jude. I'm not good at this whole vulnerability thing."

"Bullshit. You did just fine when we were talking yesterday." I push up onto my elbows and move my legs, bending at the knees to shield my groin because this is a weird conversation to have with my junk exposed.

"You didn't give me much choice," he grumbles.

"I didn't force you to tell me anything," I snap.

Theo runs a lube sticky hand through his hair, wincing when he realizes what he's done. I stifle a laugh at the way the lube mats his pretty hair. I think he might be on the verge of calling the whole thing off and running like he warned me he might. He surprises me instead. "You're right. I wanted to tell you all that. I enjoy talking to you. And if you don't want me to call you babe during sex, then I won't."

"Yeah?" I ask, jutting out my chin in challenge.

"Yeah," He confirms with a confident nod.

"Cool. So, you want to get your dick back over here and fuck me already?" I demand.

"Sure thing, Jude," Theo says as he moves over me. "Apparently you can be a bossy fucker, too," he adds, not bothering to hide his amusement.

"Guess so." I grin at him, unapologetic. Theo leans in to steal a kiss, propping himself on his elbows. He tangles his hands in my hair as our lips lock. I give an indignant squawk and shove him away.

"Jerk, now we both need to wash lube out of our hair," I whine.

"Oh, no, how tragic, we'll both need a shower when I'm done dicking you down, whatever shall we do?" Theo does a mock dramatic gesture, pressing the back of his hand to his forehead.

I give him another playful shove. He overbalances, flopping onto his back beside me.

"Hey!" Theo complains, but we're both laughing as I climb over him and take matters into my own hands, I straddle him and lower myself onto his dick. Theo grips my hips to steady me as I ride him. "Who's the bossy one now?" he teases.

I grind down on his dick at just the right angle to make myself see stars, and moan before I reply, "We already established it's both of us. Besides, you were taking too long."

"Aw, my Jude doesn't like being teased?" he quips. My movements stutter at being called his. Theo takes advantage of startling me to flip us around so he's on top again. He lifts my legs to his shoulders and fucks into me. A few experimental thrusts at first, and when that has me gasping and moaning in pleasure, he pounds into me.

I claw at his shoulders and drag him down into a kiss as he drives us both toward our climax. His hips pump into me, hard and unyielding. My orgasm seems to start in my toes and crawls up my spine to explode out of me with a hoarse shout of his name. He swallows my noises in a kiss that leaves my lips tingling with the scrape of his stubble and his teeth. I shoot my load all over my borrowed t-shirt.

Theo fucks me through it, bucking into me in wild thrusts before he shudders and comes with a broken off garbled cry. The sound is caught somewhere between my name and his usual stupid endearments. He rests his forehead against mine, his dick still a hard intrusion inside me as we catch our breath. Now that we've come, it's getting uncomfortable and I squirm. Theo winces and eases his dick out of me.

"Sorry 'bout that," Theo apologizes.

"It's fine. There are perks to being able to stay hard all night long," I give him a suggestive smile.

"Cis dicks can do that, too," Theo points out snippily as he strips the condom off his dick.

"Yeah, but if they do, it's considerably less fun," I say. I remove the t-shirt and ball it up to wipe away my mess. "Laundry?" I ask.

Theo points toward his closet, and I lean over to drop the cum covered shirt in his hamper. Theo tucks himself back into his underwear. I kind of want to check out how he attaches the prosthetic without a harness. Heck, I want to get a closer look at Theo's entire body, but he seems uncomfortable being exposed now that the sex is over. I smile up at him and stretch. His eyes rove over my body and I play up flexing.

Theo tickles my ribs. "You trying to goad me into fucking you again, Jude?"

"Much as I'd love to lie in bed with you all day, I thought you volunteered to show me the market?" I say.

"We should shower first. Ugh. You probably got my meds all over yourself. I should have stopped you from grabbing me like that."

"It's fine, Theo." I wave off his concern. "It's not like a little extra testosterone is going to hurt me."

"I guess not." He runs his fingers through his hair, grimacing at the tacky lube from earlier. "Still. All the paperwork says it can transfer to a partner if there's skin-to-skin contact and it's not ideal for you to be exposed all the time if we're doing this thing. This is reason number five thousand ninety-eight why hookups where I don't take my shirt off are easier. You should wash up with soap. Humor me?"

"If it will make you worry less, sure," I agree. I don't dignify his comment about hookups with a reply, just pull my boxers back on for the walk down the hallway.

CHAPTER 15

Theo

I hustle Jude to the bathroom. We don't encounter any of my other roommates, and I can hear Jen's music playing in her room nearest mine. Those headphones I got her for Christmas were a waste of money since she never uses them, no matter how many times I complain about her taste in music.

Once the door is closed behind us, Jude removes his underwear as I bend over the tub to turn on the water. When I turn back, Jude is eyeing me in open appreciation. I roll my eyes.

"You horny again already, b-Jude?" I tease, catching myself before I can call him babe and his smile softens.

"Just admiring the view," he replies. I can't say I mind looking at him either. This shower is a terrible idea. The adoration as he eyes me, top surgery scars and all, is dangerous for my heart. I slide my underwear down, almost daring him to flinch from my body. He doesn't react to my naked form badly. There is some curiosity, but none of the disgust that swamps me when my dysphoria is at its worst.

"So, it attaches to your underwear?" Jude asks, gesturing toward my prosthetic dick.

"Yep, the base attaches to a loop in my briefs. If you behave, I'll show you the other features later."

"What features?" Jude gives me a curious look.

"It can vibrate and shoot lube."

"Cool." Jude grins at me.

"Warm, actually," I tease. "When I wear it for a while, it gets to body temp. Unless you want me to chill the lube first?"

"Cramps for the win?" he jokes weakly.

"You want me to come inside you, Jude?" I ask, and yeah, that thought makes me hot, too. The dysphoria of knowing it's not something I can really do washes over me, but I shove it aside. I'm not sure how well the lube feature will actually work inside a person. And I never use my dicks without a condom. Not with my revolving door approach to bed partners. This one has a nice paint job I prefer to protect too. But if we're doing a relationship, I might consider it? If not when I'm topping, then when Jude's the one doing the fucking.

He makes a sound in the back of his throat, then clears it. "We should, uh, shower." He gestures toward the tub. Seems like we both like the idea of going bare. But it's way too soon for that. I fuck around too much to entertain the idea without getting tested first. Too bad lacking a cis dick offers zero protection from STIs.

I step under the water, and Jude joins me. It takes a lot longer to shower together than it would have if we took turns. But I enjoy his hands spreading soap suds over my body. And I love getting my hands on him. I'm half tempted to jerk him off with the slippery soap, but he whines about chafing after a few pumps of my fist along his length. With reluctance, I let him rinse off way before I've had my fill of his delectable uncut dick.

"You can play with it later," Jude says when I pout at him as he rinses away the soap. "Plus five to relationship sex."'

"That's more like a plus two," I argue.

"At least a plus three," Jude insists.

"Fine, plus three. You gonna roll for it?"

"Can't I do that thing where you take ten?"

"You think a ten is enough to get you laid?"

He snorts. "Hey, it's a thirteen, because of my plus three modifier. Besides, we both know you want me. I'm irresistible."

"You are something alright," I tease. The warm spray cools, the pipes rattling the way they do when the tank is running out of warm water. We don't have long before it turns frigid and I hurriedly finish rinsing myself. "It's about to get cold in here," I warn Jude. Then I duck out of the tub and wrap myself in my towel. Jude is still rinsing, and I can tell by his yelp when the last of the heated water runs dry. I dig out a fresh towel from my stack under the sink for him to dry himself.

"Poor baby," I tease. "I warned you." Jude pouts and I lean in to kiss him. It takes a monumental effort of will to tear myself away from him so we can get dressed.

After the shower, and lending Jude another clean shirt, we head out to the market. Even though I'd rather be rolling back into my bed with my—whatever Jude is to me. Boyfriend gives me hives after years of studiously avoiding the title; it still reminds me too much of Craig and the ways we hurt each other. My Jude. That has a nice ring to it.

CHAPTER 16

Jude

I'm all blissed out from my date with Theo when I return to my apartment later that afternoon. The market is closer to my place than Theo's, so I headed home after we finished our shopping and grabbed lunch at a restaurant on Granville Island.

I guess we didn't label it a date, but it was. We goofed around studying all the neat little market stalls, and Theo half-jokingly bought me a flower. To 'prove I can do that romance shit'. It was a bright purple carnation that matched his hair. I'm just as goofy in love with him as my teenage self could have imagined in my wildest fantasies. Or, if not love, that giddy first infatuated rush of having a new relationship.

I walk in the door and remove my shoes. Then, I go to take care of my flower. I wander into the kitchen for a glass to put it in water, since I don't own a fancy vase. Gui is pulling a soda out of the fridge. One look at my goofy grin and he's upset. So much for my wonderful mood.

"Oh, Jude, tell me you didn't," Gui demands. He grabs the collar of my shirt. Well, another I'd borrowed from Theo if we're being technical. The motion exposes a hickey Theo left at the base of my neck. I slap Gui's hand away.

"Hey!" I protest.

Gui raises both hands in surrender. "Sorry, but seriously, you're smarter than this, baby bro."

"Smarter than what? Letting your best friend kiss me? He's a good guy, Gui. I really like him, and he likes me. Where's the harm?" I demand.

Gui groans and massages his temples. He points an accusing finger at my single purple flower and then at my face. My expression softens as I look at the flower and remember the sweet guy handing it to me.

Theo made a big thing of playing at being gallant as he swept down onto one knee to present it to me. It was silly and sweet and his over the top wink asking me to play along with being his swooning damsel makes me smile just remembering it. I know Theo was just playing around. He enjoys teasing and being the center of attention. That sweeping romantic gesture contained a kernel of something more vulnerable, too. Something real that's been growing between us ever since our first night together.

"That expression on your face is the harm," Gui accuses. "I recognize that gleam in your eyes, Jude. You're going to get your heart broken if you give it to Theo. And he'll beat himself up over hurting you, but that won't stop him from walking away. I love you both like brothers, but this is a mistake," Gui says. He's so sincere, he truly believes that. Maybe he's even right. But I'd rather risk getting my heart broken than play it safe and miss out on something that could be great with someone I admire.

I jut out my chin and grab a glass for my flower. I open the tap with a bit too much force. The cup fills halfway before I grit out, "So what if it is? He's my mistake to make, Gui." I plop the stem into the glass, then turn on my heel to retreat to my room and away from my brother's judgment.

Laying in my bed, I text Theo.

Jude: I had fun today. We should do it again soon ;)

Jude: Gui knows about us. Sorry if he's an ass about it. I told him it's none of his business, but you know how he can get once he decides about something...

Theo: I had fun too ;-)

The next text he sends is a string of eggplant emoji and water droplets. I smile and flop onto my back, surreptitiously sniffing my shirt. It smells like Theo's laundry detergent. I'm as besotted as Gui thinks I am, but I can't bring myself to care.

Theo: I can handle your brother being an ass, but I'd rather handle yours ;)

He follows up the text with a peach emoji. I compose and delete a dozen replies to that. Nothing strikes the right balance of flirty without being overeager or desperate. Or too invested in this, so I risk spooking him into running. I sigh and settle for texting back a winking emoji. Then I bury my face in the pillows, because really? That's the best response I can come up with? Theo doesn't reply so I distract myself with a mindless game on my phone followed by a lazy nap.

Gui and Paz aren't around when I make myself dinner a while later. Something healthy with steamed veggies and grilled chicken. I've eaten out all day and I might be acting reckless in love, but I've learned the hard way to be careful about my health. On a whim, I send a food selfie to Theo and he replies with a shot of himself devouring a slice of pizza, his neon hair flopping over his eyes. I want to brush it out of his face and lick the smear of sauce off his lips.

Before I can second-guess myself, I tell him as much.

Theo: You can lick me anywhere you want, babe. ;)

Theo: *Jude, sorry, I'm working on it. ;)

Jude: Glad that you're trying. Thanks. What are you doing tonight?

Theo: My right hand?

Jude: Want to do me instead?

Oh, shit, I did not just hit send. I bite my thumb as the bouncing dots appear and disappear a few times. Should I say I'm kidding? Take it back? So much for not scaring him off with my overinvestment issues.

Theo: Spend the night again?

Jude: You sure?

Theo: I enjoy sleeping with you ;)

Theo: The sex is pretty good too ;P

Jude: Should I act insulted that it's just pretty good?

Theo: I mean, there's one surefire way to get better ;P

Jude: I'll bring a change of clothes so I don't have to keep borrowing yours.

Theo: Bring me some of Pascal's baked goods, if he's got any lying around?

Jude: I see how it is... is this a booty call or a chocolate delivery?

Theo: Why not both? *shrug* Also, Sin should totally sign up for one of those food courier services. I would pay exorbitant delivery fees to have those heavenly brownies delivered to my door.

Jude: Would you? How much is it worth to you, Theo?

Theo: I'll pay you in sexual favors, lover boy.

Jude: Hm, what kind of sexual favors?

Theo: For my very favorite chocolate vector? How about a nice sloppy blowjob and then you can finish by fucking my ass?

He punctuates that text with the chocolate bar emoji, an equal sign and then a string of eggplants and peaches. The goofball.

Theo: *sex isn't contingent on you bringing me sugary treats. If you come over, we don't have to fuck. Also, I feel like a dick now that I've thought about it for a hot second. How did I not realize you can't indulge in the chocolaty goodness that is your future brother-in-law's amazing baking?

Jude: He made me a sugar-free batch the other day. They were alright. Sweets aren't my thing. I prefer a gooey rom-com over a gooey brownie.

Theo: Well, you can have my share of the chick flicks if I can have your share of the brownies ;)

Jude: :P don't hate just because you're jealous of my excellent taste in films.

Theo: Hardly. You call yourself an animator and yet; you prefer films without so much as a single measly special effect in sight?

Jude: That can be a plus. I spend all day toiling over animation, when I watch a movie I don't want to be critiquing how it could be better or what I'd have done differently. I just want to relax and enjoy the ride.

Theo: That's acceptable. You can enjoy my ride any time ;). Are you coming over to see me?

Jude: Yeah. I'll head out after I raid the kitchen to satisfy your sweet tooth. I'll text when I arrive?

Theo: Cool. I'm a lucky boy to have my two favorite things delivered to my doorstep.

Jude: Chocolate and dick?

Theo: Oh! Jude. JUDE!!! You're a genius... Do you think they make those Candygrams, but instead of candy, it's a stripper with a chocolate dick?

Jude: Is this your way of asking me to roleplay? Because I feel like you might be into some weird ass food porn. Food goes in at the other end, Theo.

Theo: Are you kink-shaming me over my taste in porn?

Jude: Do you have a food delivery kink?

Theo: Possibly, if the food is chocolate and I get to lick it off your delectable dick.

Jude: I'll see you soon, Theo. And remember, with ass play the golden rule is: if it doesn't have a flare, don't stick it up there ;)

I check the cabinets for Pascal's latest batch of baked goods and find his triple chocolate cookies. That should satisfy my guy's sweet tooth. I snag a few to stuff into a baggie in my backpack and leave a note thanking Paz for the cookies and saying not to expect me home tonight. Or for most of the day tomorrow. Then I head out, whistling to myself. I get to see Theo again.

CHAPTER 17

17

Theo

"Hey, Jude," I serenade him as I open the door and usher my guest inside. Jen, our roommate Donna, and Donna's boyfriend are all watching sports ball on the couch.

"Holy shit, you invited the same guy home twice in a row?" Jen says. She clasps a hand to her chest like she's dying. Drama queen. I roll my eyes at her.

"Theo deigning to entertain a repeat? Is it a sign of the apocalypse?" Donna teases. Like a jerk. All my roommates are jerks.

"Did you go through every available guy in the city and have to go back for seconds, Theo?" Donna's boyfriend jokes, without glancing away from the TV.

"Seriously, guys?" I ask, mildly annoyed on my own behalf. When I glance at Jude, he seems so uncomfortable I kind of want to scream at all of them for putting that uncertainty in his expression. Most of all, I want to punch past Theo for making everything they just said totally reasonable ribbing. I am that much of a player, and it clearly freaks out my monogamy-loving hearts-and-flowers obsessed... person. My person. Not my boyfriend, that word still itches.

"Ignore these jokers," I urge Jude, tugging his arm to bring him to my room.

He lets me drag him back to my lair, but his goofy sunny smile at first seeing me is dimmer. That makes me wonder if Gui might not be right that I'm in over my head. He sent me an angry text earlier. Just after I got the one from Jude apologizing for letting the cat out of the bag. As though I expected him to lie to his brother about us. Not that it would have done much good, Gui's a smart guy and Jude stayed the night with me, then the entire next day. Plus, I make a habit of avoiding emotional commitment, so I recognized the look in Jude's eyes when I impulsively bought him a flower before we parted ways earlier. It was the same sappy look that had sent me running from every other potential relationship in my adult life.

"I'm sorry they're assholes," I apologize, running a hand through my hair and trying to collect my thoughts.

Jude shrugs and bounces on my bed. "Not your fault," he mumbles without meeting my eyes.

"Sorry they made you question this. I like you, Jude. I wouldn't intentionally hurt you," I say, imploring him to believe me.

"Yeah, I know," he says. Then he shrugs out of his backpack and pulls out a baggie with a handful of chocolate cookies. "Brought you something." He jiggles the bag in front of my face.

I stare for a moment. My heart warms that he brought

the chocolate. Sure, I'd asked him to, but I'd been mostly joking. "Thanks," I say as I take the baggie and pull out a cookie. "You didn't have to," I mumble through a mouthful of delicious baked goods, moaning as I chew. So. Fucking. Good. Gui is a lucky bastard for locking down Paz.

"Should I be jealous of Paz for making you all but come in your pants without even being present?" Jude raises an eyebrow at me.

"Not Paz, chocolate," I say, waving the cookie around. It's an important distinction. Paz is great, but he's not the one I want. I want the pretty twink in my bed.

Jude watches me devour my treat and I might play up the blissful moans and lip licking for him, just a little. He shoves me. I swallow and add, "Besides, you're the one who brought it to me, so I blame you for any choco-gasms that ensue."

"That's not a thing," he complains.

"Pft. It *so* is," I say, shooting him a cocky grin.

"Whatever, should I give you and the chocolate some privacy?" he teases.

"Jealous? Want my mouth on *you* instead?" I offer, savoring the last little bite and sucking a bit of melted chocolate chip off my finger. I hollow my cheeks and exaggerate the move.

Jude groans.

"What?" I ask, playing innocent. I even go so far as batting my lashes at him.

"Nothing," he darts his gaze away from my mouth and I grin, pouncing on him and pressing my lips to his. He goes all pliant under me, his eyes dark with lust. I let myself get lost in lingering kisses, enjoying the way he squirms against my body. I slip my chocolate free hand into his pants to play with his dick. Jude moans into my mouth as I jack him off. I love the way his foreskin glides over his cock head and along his shaft with each stroke. This is nice.

Jude makes soft little sounds of pleasure as I stroke him and kiss him and grind against his thigh. His hand cups my ass, squeezing me more firmly against him, adding the perfect amount of friction to our lazy make-out session. I could come from his touch on my body. The warmth of him in my fist, his needy movements driving me wild. I can't get enough of the slick of his pre-cum making my fingers sticky and the taste of chocolate lingering on my tongue.

"I'm close," Jude murmurs against my lips as he ruts into my hand. His gentle massaging of my ass cheek gets more insistent.

"Want to finish in my hand or my ass?" I offer. Jude bites off a moan and stills his hips. I stop stroking him, not yet removing my hand. He whines.

"Since you stopped right when I was about to blow, I'm thinking you want to get fucked?" Jude asks, there's an amused gleam in his eye.

"I can finish you this way, if you prefer?" I offer. But he's right, I want him to fuck me. I'd counted on it, getting myself ready after I invited him over.

"Nah, grab a condom?" Jude asks, sitting up.

I pull out the foil packet along with a travel size bottle of lube I stashed in my pocket earlier and toss them into his lap. Then I ditch my pants and assume the position. No underwear today, Jude's seen my junk, and he seems okay with it, no smart remarks or disgusted glances. So I can handle this. I still position myself on all fours, though. It's easier to handle intimacy when I don't have to focus on that stuff. I fish my favorite stroker out of my other pocket and get it positioned over my junk. This way I can use the suction and the textured silicone to get myself off while Jude pounds me.

"God, you've got a nice ass, Theo," Jude teases. He gives me a squeeze to emphasize his words.

"And you've got a perfect fucking dick, Jude," I shoot back. "Remind me how well my ass and your dick fit together?"

"Can I taste a bit first?" he asks as he traces a slippery finger over my hole, pressing against me, his touch featherlight. It takes my lust-addled mind a moment to process he's asking if he can rim me.

"Yeah, okay, taste fast, I want you in me," I agree. It's true—I want him to fuck me already—but it's not the whole truth. Oral stuff, at least on the receiving end, can get dicey for me. Sometimes it feels fantastic. Other times it's too much focus on my nether regions for me to bear the scrutiny, no matter how non-judgmental. It gets me lost in my head about what should be there and isn't. Yet another reason I prefer quick and dirty hookups to romance and flowers style intimacy.

"Fair's fair, I let you savor your treat," he teases, prying my cheeks apart and licking along my crack. Oh, fuck, that feels nice. The wet heat makes me squirm. I gasp his name in a strangled cry as the same sensitive stripe of flesh cools when he blows over it, sending a chill through me. Jude chuckles as he kneads my ass cheeks and moves in to nip one, then circles his tongue over my rim.

"Ngh. Oh, yeah, baby—Jude. That's nice, Jude," I let myself babble as I work the stroker. His tongue presses into me, his fingers gripping and massaging me. There's a sharp little sting where his blunt nails dig into my ass, giving me that delicious counterpoint of added sensation. I lower my chest to the bed so I can reach behind me. My fingers find his hair, just holding him against me. His head moves under my hand as he tries to undo me with his mouth on my ass.

God, that's good. My Jude is an enthusiastic lover. Not as inexperienced as I thought from our first encounter. He knows his way around a rim job, anyway. True to his word, Jude devours my ass with as much enthusiasm as I showed for my cookie and I'm floating on the bliss of it all. But I need more, need him inside me. I need him to feel good too, to make him feel as good as he's making me feel.

"I'm ready, please, get inside me, Jude. Need you inside." I drop my hand from his head.

He gently pulls away. I whine for him to hurry at the loss of his touch, but then he's kneeling behind me. Jude's hands are on my ass again, parting my cheeks as he guides his latex covered cock to my pliant rim. He fumbles a little, apologizing as his dick slides past his mark and between my thighs. He warned me he had little experience topping. Guess that's still true. He lines up better on the second attempt, pressing against me. I bear down as he penetrates me, then glides in deep. I sigh, arching into the sensation. Jude grips me hard and holds still, letting us both adjust.

"I love this," Jude breathes, his hands possessive on my flanks, his dick buried balls deep in my ass. And damn if I don't love it too, but that pronouncement is dangerously close to the other thing. I'm not ready to go there. To express emotions for him that go beyond mutual affection.

"Mm," I agree, bucking back against him. "Less talking, more fucking," I urge.

Jude lets out a heavy sigh, but he adjusts his grip and

moves to meet my thrusts. We find a quick rhythm that has the room echoing with the sounds of our pleasure. The bed creaks, flesh slaps, low moans and the wet suction of my stroker squelching as I work myself.

Jude fucks me hard, just the way I like it. It's weird to realize that he *knows* this is how I like it, that he remembers. He rubs soft circles into the small of my back with one thumb and reaches up to tangle his fingers in my hair with the other. Jude yanks me upward, so I push myself onto one elbow. He keeps up the steady pressure until I rise up to kneel in front of him. He wraps his arms around me, pinning my back to his chest as he pistons his hips, fucking me hard, though the tempo is slower at this angle.

Part of me hates how exposed I feel like this. Part of me loves being trapped against his body as he fucks into me. I work the stroker hard and fast with one hand and reach behind me to pull his face closer. Close enough that I can crane around and find his mouth. Our lips crash together as our bodies undulate, driving us both toward climax. Jude's tongue swirls against mine, and I meet his gaze, so full of unspoken emotions. He's beautiful. Sweeter than I deserve. It terrifies me, his trust and adoration. And he must see that.

Jude breaks off the kiss. His fist tangles in my hair, he jerks my face around, rough, but controlled. His breath tickles my ear as he all but growls, "Brace yourself against the wall, Theo, I want you to feel me all week."

I whimper at the words. Far too harsh to fit with the mushy expression in his eyes and just what I need to hear. Jude pulls out and I scramble into position. He grips my hip and fucks back inside of me. A few shallow thrusts to find an angle that has us both moaning, and Jude lets loose. He pummels my ass like there's no tomorrow and I rock back to meet each stroke. He squeezes my ass, pulling my cheeks apart to get that slight bit deeper.

"Smack it," I demand, so fucking close.

Jude hesitates. And then he slams into me, his palm cracking over my ass cheek with a loud smack. Perfect.

I cry out in ecstasy.

"Again," I plead. Jude does it again. One hand slaps my ass, the other pulls my hair. He yanks my face around for another brutal clash of teeth and tongue as he devours me in a scorching, ardent kiss. His hips snap hard against me. I grind into the stroker, tipping over the edge of release. My muscles clench hard around Jude's perfect dick as I fly off into bliss.

"Fuck, you're so tight, so good, Theo, so close," Jude babbles. And then he's crying my name as he pumps his load into the condom, buried inside my ass.

CHAPTER 18

18

Jude

I wake up in Theo's bed again. It's hazardous to my heart how happy that makes me. This is the fourth weekend in a row that I haven't slept in my room. Theo and I ate lunch together almost every day these past few weeks. We've sent countless inane messages to each other on a private chat all throughout the work week. We even got together for dinner a couple times. I fell asleep in his bed streaming a movie on Wednesday night. He didn't wake me up, so I had to wear one of his shirts to work on Thursday. The grin on his face every time he glimpsed it on me was enough to make me want to steal his clothes every day.

I'm falling hard for him. The sort of love I always dreamed about, like what my parents had. I remember them dancing together in the kitchen when they cooked our dinner, or having a fight with soap suds in the sink instead of washing the dishes.

I remember them singing to each other in the car, Dad taking on an awful falsetto and Mom giggling when his voice broke over the high notes. It used to embarrass me when they sang along with the radio while they drove me places with my friends. I'd give anything to hear them serenade me in just one last terrible off key act of musical butchery.

They smiled just from being in each other's company. They shared all these little in-jokes that made them giggle. When they were together, it was like the rest of the world didn't matter. I was part of their love, but it was also just for them. Above all else, I want that same all-consuming love for myself.

Gui is like that with Paz. My big brother lights up when he's around his boyfriend. They haven't been together long, but I see the love in his eyes. The way they turn toward each other, like flowers seeking the light.

That's how I look at Theo, when he sings my name like I make him brim over with too much happiness to contain. Like his brightness is the only light I need. He'd freak if I told him a tenth of that, so I keep the words to myself. It's way too soon for declarations of love, no matter how heartfelt they may be.

I nuzzle into his neck, and his arms tighten around me. For all that he fears letting me into his heart, he's a snuggle monster. I enjoy the way his mostly naked body feels pressed against mine. Other than Theo putting his shirt back on, we didn't bother with clothes after our super hot frottage last night.

"Mm," Theo mumbles into my hair. "Morning."

"Morning," I reply, enjoying his arms around me. Theo gives me one more squeeze, then squirms free of me.

"Gotta pee," Theo explains. He throws back the blankets, letting the chill into our warm cocoon. I'm not sure if it's true, or an excuse to get up and get distance. "Shower and breakfast?" Theo suggests. He perches on the edge of his bed to pull on a pair of lounge pants before opening his door. I reach into my overnight bag to get dressed, too. Theo leans in to kiss me, heedless of my morning breath. He keeps it sweet, pulling away to grin at me. There's an echo of my own intense emotions in his eyes as he smiles down at me.

"Shower, then food sounds good," I agree. Theo grabs my bag for me and we pad down the hallway to the bathroom. I test my morning sugar before indulging in a heated exchange of shower BJs with Theo.

When we're ready for the day, we make breakfast. He has whole wheat pancake mix and turkey sausages in his kitchen. We bought them together last Sunday, opting to do groceries instead of brunch out again.

We cook together, and it's a pleasant way to start the day right until Jen wanders in and starts teasing Theo. Again.

"Good morning, Theo and Jude," Jen greets us. Then she chuckles to herself as she shuffles around us to make coffee.

"What?" Theo asks, defensive.

"Nothing. It's just so weird to know the name of one of your tricks. And now he's got you downright domesticated," Jen gestures to our food. Theo bristles. The tension in his body as he scowls at his roommate is obvious. I plate up the last pancake and all the sausages.

"It's not like that," Theo argues through gritted teeth.

Jen gestures between us. "Sure, and Jude doesn't have you by the balls. It's cool, Theo. You don't have to go tomcatting around to prove your manliness."

"What's that supposed to mean?" Theo snaps.

Jen raises her hands in a warding off gesture. "Chill. Just saying, it's strange to see you settled down. No shade or anything. Touchy much?"

"Let's just eat," I suggest. Theo is scowling, but he snatches up his plate and grabs my hand to lead me into the living room where we eat crouched awkwardly over the low coffee table.

"Sorry," Theo grumbles into his plate.

"Don't worry about it," I brush off the encounter. We eat in tense silence.

"We're still on for a video game night at my place?" I check. Gui was the one who invited him over to play, along with the rest of our gaming group, so I figure Theo won't cancel. It's still a relief when he nods and pats my thigh.

"Of course. Wouldn't miss it. Pia is bringing her family."

"I still haven't met baby Rain yet," I say.

"What about Emil and Gregor?" Theo asks.

"No, just Pia, when we all went out bar hopping a few weeks back," I say, forking up a bite of pancake.

Theo gives me a heated look. Is he also remembering that was the night we hooked up in the club's back alley? I ended up buying Max a week of lunches to pay off our bet.

"Ah," Theo says with a slight frown. "Well. That wasn't Pia's best night. They haven't gotten many chances to go out sans baby."

"The kid is adorable, based on the pictures I've seen. Um, speaking of, is the kid a girl or a boy?" I ask. "They always just call the baby by name. Or say they?"

Theo ruffles my hair. "When we asked at our group

baby shower, Pia told us, 'unless you're changing the kid's diapers, you don't need to know about Rain's genital configuration.' The three of them are using they/them pronouns until Rain is old enough to pick for themself." He shrugs.

"That's cool. Better than forcing stereotypes on them, right?" I ask.

"Yeah. I guess. I'm no expert on kids. Emil will talk your ear off about various child rearing philosophies and early development, if you let him. He was a preschool teacher, so he's into that stuff."

"Was?" I ask, curious

"Yeah, he teaches grade six now." Theo elaborates.

"Cool."

"Yep, dude adores that tiny baby. I'm pretty sure he'd have about a dozen more if Gregor and Pia were cool with it."

"Are they not?" I ask. Not that it's any of my business, I barely know the trio.

Theo shrugs. "Dunno. Pia's chafing at staying home with the little sprite. I think the plan was for her to take the full year, but I doubt they'll stay away from work that long."

"Oh. Why isn't Emil taking their parental leave, then? That's a thing here, right?" I ask, curious because it's different from what I'm familiar with. Not that I had much experience with pregnant people. But I'd seen yearlong mat leave job vacancies posted on job boards when I made my plans to follow Gui up to Canada.

Theo waves his hand around as he explains, "Legal shit, I guess? Emil mentioned an issue with getting all three of them on the birth certificate, when they were trying to do it online. I think they got it resolved? You'd have to ask them for the specifics, but I wouldn't. I think it's a sore spot." He rubs the back of his neck sheepishly. Knowing Theo, he realized that after asking intrusive questions about the issue. He's not the best at thinking before he speaks sometimes.

"That... really fucking sucks," I say. It sucks with the same sort of bleak powerlessness I'd felt when I'd been old enough to understand that loving boys meant I might not have the same legal rights to my partner or kids that other people took for granted.

I'd been fifteen when that changed, and I wasn't even ashamed to admit that I cried about it the day I heard. Happy-mad tears because it should have always been true and because it meant I could have the life that I'd always dreamed of.

"Yeah. It does," Theo nods. "I could be wrong about their reasons. Pia didn't want to talk about it. Did I tell you I got doused in gross baby fluids when they went into labor? We were having lunch together, and she popped like a freaking water balloon. I mean, they'd been having contractions most of the day, so we expected it was almost baby time, but I didn't expect it all over my lunch." He gestures with his syrupy fork as he talks.

"Why are we discussing amniotic fluid over breakfast?" I ask him, because thinking about it makes my insides all squirmy.

"Because, I had to suffer through having it all over my shoes while I was eating my soup, so everyone else should at least hear about my traumatic birth experience?" Theo licks his fork, then waves it at my plate. "Finish your breakfast, we can swing by Game Citadel on our way to your place for games."

"Why would we do that?" I ask. "Also, I don't think

being next to someone in labor counts as a traumatic birth experience."

"There was amniotic fluid practically in my soup: it counts. And we're going because I want to pick up some new card expansion packs for Spectral. I figure, there aren't enough controllers to all play on the PlayStation." Theo stretches and the bare strip of his torso when his shirt rides up distracts me. He notices, and winks at me, that cocky grin on full display. "So we can run a friendly round robin of Spectral, too. That way everyone can play."

"I haven't played trading card games since Gui moved to Canada," I hedge. Not that I don't enjoy games, just that most of my school friends weren't into children's card games.

"Don't worry about it, we'll play on teams." Theo grins at me as he squeezes my knee. "I have some killer decks. Stick with me and we'll kick Gui and Paz's asses."

"I know all about your killer dicks..." I joke.

Theo guffaws and brushes his floppy purple curls out of his eyes. "Always happy to oblige with a hands-on demonstration, if you need a closer look," he offers with a goofy eyebrow waggle. I lean in and kiss him, because he's cute when he's trying to be all seductive. "Is that a yes to morning sex?" Theo asks when I release his face.

I glance at the time on my phone. "We have time for a quickie, want me to blow you?" I offer.

Theo's expression turns lusty, but he gestures at my half-finished plate. "Eat up first."

I snort. "Better eat up before I eat your ass out? You're being awful bossy about what I put in my mouth this morning, Theo."

"Yeah, and you love it, hun. Now, put it in your

mouth," Theo directs me with a flirty wink. And the new endearment doesn't bother me. It feels genuine, not like he's using it to distance me. I grin at him, making a show of devouring the rest of my pancake.

CHAPTER 19

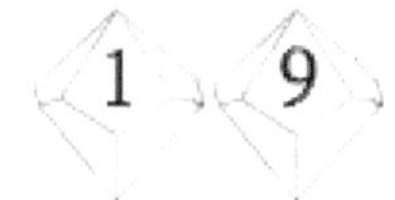

Theo

Jude and I arrive at Gui's place early. I figure it's better this way. The extra time before the others arrive should give Gui a chance to air his grievances with me in private. I've been low-key avoiding him since he found out about my thing with Jude.

This whatever it is we're doing where I invite Jude to sleep in my bed on the weekends and think about him when we're apart. Text him when I go to bed and when I wake up, or just because he's on my mind. Where I buy a plushy cartoon rabbit cereal mascot keychain for him at the game shop because he worked on a commercial for the cereal brand during his internship. The rabbit's stupid fuzzy face makes me think of him.

Shit. I know what that is. That's mushy hearts and flowers and rainbows romance crap. I don't do true love. I don't do relationships.

Except Jude's different. The way he laughed and kissed

my cheek, all delighted with the gift when I gave him the key chain, made my heart melt. He makes me want to try that stuff I packed up and swore off when Craig threw my scariest, worst thoughts back in my face. Jude listens to me. He sees me.

But I thought love and trust meant I could share everything with someone before. And Craig burned me. I swore I'd never let anyone else have the chance to hurt me that deeply ever again. I don't like the way I reacted to that hurt either. Craig suffered from my retaliating by ostracizing him from our friends.

I fidget nervously outside the apartment door. Jude stops fumbling with the ridiculous rabbit keychain symbol of how far I've fallen for him and squeezes my hand.

"He won't be mad at you, Theo," Jude assures me. He gives my hand a sympathetic squeeze. It would be easy to roll with his assumption. I *am* concerned about Gui's reaction to seeing this thing between Jude and I up close. My avoidance of talking about Jude and my relationship with Gui has gone on for weeks now, no easy feat when we had our game last week. But the thought that has me standing here looking poleaxed is the realization that I'm already in the danger zone. Head over heels for the sweet boy holding my hand, and it terrifies me.

"Thought I heard people in the hallway," Gui exclaims as the door flies open, startling me and making me jump and drop Jude's hand. Gui glances slyly between us. "Am I interrupting something?"

"Don't razz him, you'll scare him off," Jude complains. He tugs on my elbow and I let him lead me inside, even though my sense of self-preservation tells me to run. Run away and never return. *Snort. That line never gets old.* Gui is watching me, arms crossed and a knowing glint in his eyes.

"You sure I haven't scared him off already?" Gui jokes. He claps me on the back.

I try to relax.

"Jealous I picked the cuter brother?" I tease as Jude and I kick off our shoes and hang up our jackets.

Gui shoves me. "Don't be an ass, we're both hot stuff. And don't think you can distract me; we *are* discussing this." He points between Jude and me accusingly.

"I'll just go put my stuff away and let you two have a private BFF chat," Jude says. He takes the bag from the store out of my hands and pecks me hard on the lips before darting off to his room. I stare after him, helplessly, hopelessly in love.

Gui claps an arm around my shoulders and guides me in the opposite direction, to the kitchen. "Want a brownie? Paz made a pan of them for today. He should be home from his half-shift soon."

"Um, yeah. You know I never refuse Paz's baking," I agree, confused that he's acting like there's nothing wrong. Gui nods and turns to grab a plate. I thought I pissed him off. By ignoring his messages, if nothing else. "Aren't you mad at me?"

Gui puts a slice of gooey chocolate perfection on the plate along with a fork and slides it to me. "I'm not mad. I wasn't sure what to think when Jude told me you were dating. Sure, the idea that you two might hurt each other upset me, but Paz helped me cool down and convinced me it's not for me to decide who either of you date. Besides, it's obvious you truly are smitten. Never thought I'd see the day."

I clutch the fork halfway to my mouth, and gape at him. "I'm not..."

Gui laughs. Actually *laughs* at me. "You are so in *lurv* with him. Don't even play. I've seen the cup of flowers in his room."

So I'd been buying Jude flowers on our lunch break each day this week. It isn't a big deal. Just a single purple flower a day to add to his collection. It makes him smile and I love that smile. Doesn't mean I love *him*. Except I think I'm already headed down that primrose path, running at breakneck speed toward what can only be inevitable heartbreak, right? My face falls and I see the concern in Gui's expression.

"What?" he asks.

"Oh, fuck." I set the fork down and bury my face in my hands, because I'm going to hurt Jude. It's inevitable. It's also the last thing I want to do. "I fucked up so hard, Gui."

Gui's arms wrap around me and he says, "I don't think you have, Theo. Tell me what's wrong?" He holds me at arm's length to search my face.

"I'm falling for him." I admit, scrubbing at my eyes even though I'm not crying. Not yet, I've got that tight hot sensation behind my eyes, like there're tears there waiting to fall, but I can't quite get to them yet.

"Why is that a bad thing?" Gui asks, puzzled.

"You know why! I'm not what he deserves. He's all epic romance and sweet gestures and I'm a fucked up mess."

"You're not. And Jude has been floating on cloud nine all week. He was babbling on about how you stocked up on healthy food for him to eat at your place, and the flowers and the silly memes you've been sending him. He's barely been home."

"Yeah, and what do you think will happen the next time my depression gets bad? When I can't live up to the sweet doting boyfriend image he has in his head?" I demand. This isn't the time to raise my voice. I'm talking too loud, I always talk too loud. "When I can hardly drag my ass out of bed and face going to work, let alone give him what he expects. How will that work?"

Gui opens his mouth to reply, but before he can, Jude's soft voice makes me spin to face him. He's leaning on the kitchen doorframe. I grimace, knowing my panicky raised voice drew him to intervene.

"If you get that sad, then I'll be there with you, Theo," Jude says. He looks hesitant, standing at the threshold to the kitchen. Like he's not sure if he's intruding. But there's a fierceness to his expression that belies the timid posture. "If getting out of bed is too much some days, then I'll stay with you under the covers. And if your negative thoughts get too loud, I'll help you drown them out. Whatever you need, I want to be there for you. Like you stood by me when I had that hypo at the club. You took care of me. Why do you assume I wouldn't do the same for you?"

I shake my head in denial.

"You had a bad hypo?" Gui demands, stepping toward Jude. As though a past episode is something he can protect his brother from. Jude rolls his eyes.

"It wasn't bad, and Theo made sure I was safe." Jude brushes his brother's concern aside. He comes to me. "That's what you do when you care about someone, Theo. You love them even when things are bad, or they're sick, or depressed. You love them even when they can't love themself. And I love you, Theo. Enough to believe in us."

"I, uh, Jude..." I shake my head, not sure what I'm denying, but this is too much. It's all too much, and it's moving too fast. The vicious voice whispering in the back of my mind tells me I should run, that I'll never be good enough for Jude. I'll always remain stuck as that broken, scared boy pleading for help and understanding. And instead getting shoved closer to the edge of a despair so big it threatens to devour me whole.

Craig used to say he loved me, too. He used to say he loved me no matter what. When I came out to him, he said he still loved me, no matter who I was inside. But that had been a lie. Sure, he'd accepted me as a boy, but when I let him see my hopelessness, he'd turned away.

Jude isn't Craig. I know that, but it isn't enough to overcome my fear that he'll react the same way when he sees how bad I can get. Even with the antidepressants I've tried, and the hormones and surgeries that make my body feel more like my own and less like some sort of hostile cage I'm trapped inside, I still have days where I want to give up. They've been few and far between since I came out, but they still happen.

I swallow hard and search for the right words. Instead, when I open my mouth, the wrong words tumble out. "I don't think I can handle this."

Gui glares at me. Jude's soft smile crumples, but he still has a fierce, stubborn expression on his face.

"Then I'll wait until you can," Jude insists. "I'll care enough for both of us. If you want to pump the brakes, we can. But I'll still care about you, Theo. Even if we aren't dating. Or you decide we can't sleep together anymore, or if you go back to fucking any guy with a pulse. I'll care if you run away to lick your wounds. And I'll care even if you don't return my feelings, or the words are too scary for you to say them back."

"Jude, I—" I shake my head, unable to summon up the words.

"I love you, Theo. I know it's fast. It's okay if you aren't there yet. It's not a transaction and you don't have to earn it. I just love you. I don't expect that to change anything between us, but I want you to know. Now, eat your brownie, and get ready to kick some asses. You promised me a round robin tournament victory, and I intend to collect. So whip out your big bad decks and let's show everyone how it's done," Jude demands.

He winks at me. And yeah, I fucking love him, too. It's big. Scary. Way too much for me to handle only three weeks after giving in to this maddening pull between us that we've been dancing around since our first night together. Three weeks of spending every spare moment together, only parting to go to work or spend the occasional night alone. But maybe scary is okay. Better than okay, even.

The emotional intimacy I've been sharing with Jude from the start is more than I've had with anyone else. Even on our first night together, he shared pieces of himself with me. Details that went beyond the sex. He told me about his folks and how much he misses them. It's easy to love him when he makes me feel seen. Not just the flashy facade, either. When Jude says he loves me, I believe he means every part of me, even the insecure bits.

"Well, when you put it like that, I wouldn't want to let my partner down," I say with false bravado. "And no, I don't want anyone else in my bed. Only you, hun." I mean that with all my heart. Only him. He's the only one I want to call by endearments anymore.

Jude squeezes my bicep, and the understanding in his expression softens the tension in my belly. I love this man. I can't say it with words, not yet, but I say it with the searing kiss I pull him into. Tasting him because he's better than even the world's best brownies. I say it with the flowers and silly gifts. With the daily check-ins. The way I hold his hand in front of all our friends and co-workers and claim him as mine. And somehow, that's enough for him. It gives me hope that I might be enough, too.

CHAPTER 20

2 0

Jude

It's game day again. A week since I opened my big mouth and risked everything by saying the L-word to Theo. He hasn't said it back, but I'm pretty sure if he didn't share my feelings, he'd have run for the hills after that. Sunday marks a month since we agreed to try this dating thing, so I've got plans for us.

I'm nervous about spooking Theo if I make too big of a deal about it, but I want to acknowledge the milestone. I won't have an epic Spectral round robin tournament victory to shift the focus with if pointing out the occasion is too much for him to handle, though.

Last weekend, our victory distracted him from my sappy love declaration enough that he relaxed about kissing me in front of everyone after we crushed Laura and Errol. Errol's attrition deck annoyed the crap out of Theo, but my man's big beefy monster combos were enough to pull out a victory for us, as promised.

Theo's been buzzing about tonight's VentureQuest session all day. Since it's the first Friday of the month, he's decked out in a shark onesie pajama thing for dollar donation day. The protruding fin on the back thwacked Errol in the face no less than a dozen times on the walk over to his favorite sushi restaurant for lunch, much to Errol's exasperation. The teeth lining the hood flopped around Theo's face as he gestured excitedly over our meal. I suspect he chose the restaurant because it amused him to devour raw fish while dressed as a shark.

He has something fun up his sleeve for tonight's game and it's cute how excited that makes him. He and Max went for a coffee break together around three, so I figure we'll be running into more of Maximus Powers's shenanigans.

We're getting a new party member tonight too, since Pia returned to work early. Effective last Monday. I guess they worked out whatever issues were keeping Emil from watching their cute as fuck baby. Rain attended our game day last weekend, too. Strapped to Emil's chest in a baby carrier for most of the visit, though Laura and Errol demanded baby cuddles.

I'd snapped a photo of Theo playing with the infant on a blanket on the ground, and it kind of made my heart do a weird wobbly thing. But that's jumping way ahead of myself. Theo doesn't want kids of his own and he can't even bring himself to say the words 'I love you'.

Not that I need to hear them. It's obvious he cares about me. He might still struggle with saying it, but no one outside my family has ever made me feel as cared for. Theo holds my hand in public, loud and proud of being with me. He gives me silly sweet gifts. He shares his thoughts with me. That's priceless. I know how much it costs him to talk about his emotions with me. How his baggage makes it hard for him to open up. So he might not have said it in so many words, but I know he returns my feelings.

Gui and I go to Sin and Chocolate to pick up drinks for everyone before our game session begins. Paz greets my brother with fuck me eyes. He already has our entire group's drink order ready to go in two cardboard beverage carriers.

"I threw in a couple of our sugar-free low carb peanut butter cookies for you, Jude," Paz says, once he and Gui finish being lovey-dovey.

"Thanks, man. You didn't have to put yourself to any trouble," I say. I don't have anywhere near Theo and Gui's level of sweet tooth, but it's still a kind gesture.

Paz snorts, "I wanted to make you something. Everyone deserves a bit of indulgence, right? Anyway, I'm trying new recipes and they're sweet with a savory twist, and low glycemic index. I stuck the nutrition facts from the recipe on the label, so let me know what you think."

"I'll let you know," I promise with a grin. Gui pays for our order and says his goodbyes. My phone buzzes with a message from Theo.

Theo: Hey, where are you? I can't wait to start, hurry!

Jude: I went with Gui to help him carry your daily offering of chocolate. How else am I supposed to buy my GM's favor?

I almost type 'buy your love' but think better of it at the last moment. That's still too raw to tease him about it.

Theo: I can suggest some ideas... ;) Maybe we can work

out a boyfriend buff table. I'll give you a +1 to dex for a hand job, +1 to charisma for BJs, +1 strength for fucking me, +1 con for letting me fuck you, kisses for +1 initiative...

Jude: Good deal, maybe I should share this table with Errol, bet he'd blow you for a charisma buff. ;P

Theo: Um, no. That offer is only available to you. You may have heard the only one buffing me these days is my cute as hell BF.

Jude: So, is this retroactive? How do I collect? And are we sharing the chart with the group, cause I think the party might notice my sudden godlike strength. ;)

Theo: You're a dragon, I think the strength goes without saying.

Theo: Okay, fine. No favoritism just because you're my BF. Get back here with my chocolate now, plz.

Theo: Blah. Laura, Max, and Errol are here with dinner. Want me to nuke your meal, too?

Jude: I'll eat later. Want to keep my usual schedule. We'll be back soon.

Gui is watching me with a bemused smile as I stuff the phone back in my pocket to take the second drink tray and bag of pastries.

"What?" I ask.

"Nothing. Was Theo asking where we are?" Gui guesses.

"Yeah," I reply.

"You two are still good?" he checks.

"Yep," I agree.

"Good. I'm glad for you, Jude. I'm sorry I acted like a prick about you seeing him. Guess I was wrong to say you were a terrible match."

"You were," I say, not sugar-coating it. Gui should have known his best friend better. Theo might seem like a superficial fuckboy, but the guy under that facade cares deeply about the people in his life. And Gui is one of those people. He ought to have realized Theo isn't as unaffected as he pretends to be. That's between Gui and Theo. It's not my business to interfere in their friendship. Rather than dwell on it, I change the subject.

"Hey, I had a question about *Dreamer 2*, do you think when *Battle Fox* wraps in the next couple months, I might transfer over to your project?"

"It's a possibility. I can check with Errol, I could use a couple more juniors on cycles for some mobs."

"Cool. Monster cycles sound fun."

"Fun," Gui laughs, "Sure kid, keep telling yourself that."

I scowl at him. "I think they're fun, just because you're old and jaded…"

"So old. Ancient compared to you," Gui agrees, then in his best old geezer voice he adds, "back in my day…"

We exchange grins and bump each other's shoulders. Pia comes down from the third floor as Gui and I are keying into the animation department where the conference room we use is located.

"Hey," Gui greets them with a hug. I wave. Pia smiles wide. We chat as we walk toward the conference room, Gui asks how Pia feels about coming back to work this week.

"You have no idea how happy I am to be getting back to my adult life," Pia says with a toothy grin. She pushes open the door and proclaims, "I'm back bitches! Also, Gui, don't get me wrong, I love Rain, but it is incredible to be back at work. I almost forgot what it was like spending time with people who talk instead of just puking all over me."

"Well, I'd be more than happy to puke on you a little, if you get nostalgic," Theo offers, his voice carrying. He winks at Pia. "I owe you after the water breaking incident."

Pia flips him off.

"Love you too, Pea," Theo makes a kissy-face at them.

Pia rolls her eyes, then walks around the table to give Theo a hug. "Trust me, if I'd known you'd hold such a grudge about it, I'd have aimed to hit more than just your shoes."

"Gross!" Theo exclaims. "That mental image has scarred me for life," he declares, one hand thrown theatrically against his brow. "Can people actually aim that stuff? Blech, no, don't tell me. I don't want to know."

"It's not something you can control, Theo," Laura says. She rolls her eyes, exasperated by his antics. "You can't just hold in amniotic fluid like pee."

"Technically, it's baby pee, right?" Max asks, his tone innocent, but his smirk giving away that he's stirring the pot.

"Why are we talking about childbirth?" Errol asks, but his tone implies he's beseeching the heavens rather than any of us.

"I'm with Max on this one," Theo agrees. "We should allow the miracle of life to remain shrouded in mystery."

"If you'd paid attention in your health classes..." Errol starts, pushing his glasses up his long nose.

"La-la-la-la," Theo stuffs his fingers in his ears and

sticks out his tongue at Errol.

"Are we ready to start?" I ask to shift the focus. The banter is light and playful, but I recognize the look in Theo's eyes. That little spark of panic he gets on the days he doesn't want me to look at his junk when I fuck him. This conversation is upsetting him.

"We come bearing chocolate," Gui adds, picking up on my cue to change the subject. We hold up the cardboard trays, and everyone grabs their drinks. Gui ordered something for Pia that has her moaning in pleasure to rival Theo's sex sounds over his hot cocoa.

"I can't remember the last time I got to have a mocha mint macchiato from Sin. Infinitely better than the decaf crap I've endured for months." Pia says.

"Better than sex," Theo agrees. He gives me a broad wink.

"Hey!" I protest. "See if you're getting laid tonight."

"Ugh, TMI!" Gui groans.

"Seconded," Errol agrees. "Also, you two are perfect together; I hate it."

"Sorry, Jude, but my tastebuds are sluts for chocolate," Theo blusters.

"You're a—" I start to retort, but Max cuts me off.

"And that's enough flirting. Come on, people, let's get this show on the road, before the minions of evil tire of babysitting a dragonling and straight-up murder the dragon prince," Max demands. He crosses his arms and glares.

Theo winks at me and mouths, 'later.' We take our seats and dive into sleuthing out Sythern's kidnappers' trail. Maximus appears again. This time he's consorting with a dread necromancer who is terrorizing a tiny village. The village is in the foothills of the merc group's mountain fortress. A closer review reveals that the necromancer had spell parts Maximus needed. So he took them. His avarice broke the necromancer's control over a passel of wraiths.

We break through the necromancer's terrible wards only to discover that her thralls have slipped their leash. The monsters devoured her magic, leaving her powerless to free her young apprentice who got trapped inside their tower's magical wards. Freed of any control, the thralls attacked the town. Turns out, the apprentice is Pia's new character. We help her escape the tower. In return, she helps us dispel her mentor's escaped thralls to rescue the villagers.

Pia gets really into character, they're a fun addition to the group. The two of us come up with an interesting little plot to get back at Maximus for his interference in her mentor's domain. Something we devise by passing notes so the rest of the group won't interfere. I'm excited to spring our trap next session.

It's a fun night. We run late enough that no one is up for drinks afterward, everyone eager to get home. Pia seems disappointed about that, but their jaw-cracking yawn belies their protestations of not being ready to head home yet.

"I'm bushed, but let me know if you three need a sitter again," Laura reminds Pia.

"We'll definitely take you up on that sometime soon," Pia agrees.

"Come on, I'll drive you, we can grab drive-thru shakes on the way," Errol offers, tucking Pia under his arm. "You need a ride, Laura?"

"Yeah, I'll tag along, thanks, I hate taking the SkyTrain out to the 'burbs alone late at night," Laura shivers.

"Happy to be of service." Errol winks at her. "Catch the rest of you on Monday."

"See you all on Monday," Pia echoes. "We need to do a group lunch to celebrate my triumphant return from the land of constant puke, poop, and pee. Burgers all around!"

We all agree to lunch and say our goodbyes. Errol walks Pia and Laura outside.

"Everything good with the guys, Pia?" I overhear him asking just before the door closes behind them.

Max watches them leaving, then says, "That was fun. I'm glad we worked this whole player BBEG thing out, Theo."

"I mean, you're not quite the big bad, evil guy, but close enough," Theo winks at him as he gathers up his crap. Somehow Theo has spread his belongings over every surface of the conference room.

"You coming home tonight, bro?" Gui asks me from the doorway.

I give him a sheepish look, then glance toward Theo. "Am I going home with you?" I ask my boyfriend.

Theo darts a glance up from the dice he's stuffing back into his bag and muttering to himself. "Huh? I'm missing my lucky unicorn D20." He frowns, and sorts through the stuff still spread over the table.

Gui chuckles. "You're hopeless, Thee." He strides forward and plucks the missing die off the filing cabinet behind Theo's chair where he must have set it earlier. Theo heaves a relieved sigh, "Thanks. Um, did you say something, Jude?"

Max snorts. "He asked if you're down to fuck."

"Hey! Don't be crude," Gui smacks Max on the back of the head gently.

"I asked if you wanted company tonight," I rephrase.

Max is only partially right. I want to screw around, but I'd be just as happy to snuggle and fall asleep together, wake up in the same bed with Theo wrapped around me.

"Nope, just you, hun." He winks and I stick out my tongue at him. Gui rolls his eyes.

"Catch you lovebirds Monday," Gui teases.

"You're just as bad as we are," Theo shoots back.

"Gah, you all are surrounding me with your love cooties, no fair," Max complains.

"So, you want me to come over?" I ask, awkward as fuck.

"Duh." Theo gives me a puzzled glance. "Do you need to ask? I figured you were coming home with me. When was the last Friday you didn't stay over?" Theo asks as he jams his game books back into his bag, then stuffs the pouches of dice and little resin figures into the front pocket. He flips on his hood before donning the bag.

"This will mark five weeks," I reply without hesitation. A month of weekends curled up in his bed.

Theo blinks, considers, then grins. "It's been a month? Is this our monthiversary? Shit," his face falls, "was I supposed to get you something?"

"No, you big goofball, you don't have to get me anything," I press a kiss to his lips, the shark teeth on his hood framing our faces.

"And that's our cue to leave, Maximus. Text me if I should expect you home before Sunday night, Jude," Gui says with a smirk.

"I will," I assure him. "You and Paz have fun with the apartment to yourselves."

"Oh, we will," Gui agrees with a broad wink, getting me back for my TMI about Theo and my sex life earlier in the evening. He slings an arm around Max and the two of them leave Theo and I alone.

"Phew, good. About the gifts. Cause I'd get you such an amazing gift you'd feel bad about your paltry offering of chocolate and that would just be sad." Theo winks. He surveys the room to be sure he has everything. The action figures from his desk that represented the wraiths we fought somehow ended up under his chair. So I grab them for him, stepping close enough to steal another kiss as I hand them to him.

"Thanks, guess I need to stop by my desk on the way out. You ready?"

"Yeah," I clear my throat, not making any move to leave. "I, uh, got us something to try off Etsy. If you want."

"Yeah?" Theo grins at me. He steps into my personal space and presses his thigh between my legs. "Is it something NSFW?"

"It is," I agree, swatting his ass. "We shouldn't fool around in the conference room."

"Why not?" Theo pouts.

"Aren't there security tapes?" I ask, glancing up toward the camera mounted in a corner of the room.

"Eh? Who watches those?" Theo dismisses my concerns.

"Someone might," I insist. "Come on, I'd rather take our time at home."

"Spoilsport." Theo sighs dramatically, but he leads me toward the exit without further ado.

CHAPTER 21

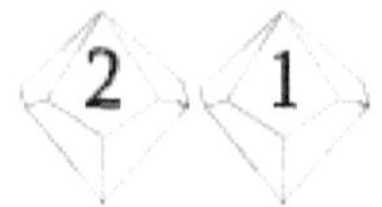

Theo

When we get back to my place, Jude's gift cracks me up as soon as I pull it out of the paper bag he hands me. Chocolate lube, an edible chocolate jock type thing, some sort of glittery body chocolate, and a chocolate dick lollipop.

"Oh, my god!" I say through peels of laughter. "I fucking love you, you big dork," I blurt. And then I freeze and dart my eyes to his face. The joy there is radiant and I can't take it back. We sit staring at each other. Then Jude tackles me onto my bed and devours my mouth in a scorching kiss. He ruts against me.

"I love you too, Theo," he tells me as I hump against his erection. We both groan at the friction, and we lose ourselves in each other until Jude rolls on top of me and demands that I try out my gifts. "It's definitely naked time, don't you want to try your gifts?"

I reach for the candy and he swats it out of my hand.

"That one is for later," he grouses.

So I grab the jock and hold it toward him with an eyebrow waggle. "Shall I eat this off your delectable dick then, lover boy?" I tease.

"Yeah. You should definitely do that." Jude agrees, nodding his head. It takes a minute for us both to strip and for me to tear through the packaging and get the chocolate wrapped around his package. I grin up at him once it's in place.

"Should I just leave that there to melt into your pubes?" I suggest. The scent of his skin mingled with chocolate as I nuzzle into his thigh is weirdly intoxicating. I'm not even close to ready to eat the stuff, though.

I reach for the body glitter, dipping a finger into the tub with an artsy handmade looking label and painting a racing stripe along his dick. The mixture is tacky on my fingers, but the gold glitter is pretty. Jude jerks and bucks into my touch with a low moan. "This is fun. I kind of want to finger paint all over you."

"Do it," he encourages, lust in his eyes. I doodle a smiley face over his happy trail. Jude chuckles. So I keep playing with him. I draw a flower around his navel and a cartoonish pirate under his left nipple.

Jude squirms when I hit a ticklish spot and snorts out a laugh when I complete the pirate with a little bird on his shoulder.

"Why is there a pirate pointing his hook at my nipple?" Jude demands.

"Dunno. Cause he's looking for booty?" I tease, groping his ass. Jude lets out a startled yelp of laughter and I roll onto him to pin him in place as I lick the glittery chocolate pirate off his chest. It actually tastes pretty fucking awful and I gag, abandoning my efforts to touch and tease

Jude in favor of getting that foul flavor out of my mouth.

"Ew, that's rank," I exclaim, much to Jude's amusement. He laughs as I scrub my hand over my tongue, trying to claw the glittery false chocolate off my tastebuds. When my efforts fail at erasing the terrible taste, I crawl up Jude's body and lick into his mouth. He stops laughing and splutters at me as I kiss him with way more tongue than is necessary.

"Ugh, gross. Uncle! You were right," he wails through laughter as he tries to fend me off. I let him push me away once I've shared the misery. Jude scrubs at his mouth with the back of his hand. "Blech, you're getting that toxic chocolate lie all over everything now," he gripes.

"Hey, you're the one who bought it. This was inevitable," I gesture to the brown and gold glitter smeared over both our torsos after I squirmed my way up his body.

Jude sighs. "It was sexier in my head. Maybe chocolate brown wasn't the best color choice. It looks like we're smeared in glittery feces," he laments.

I wrinkle my nose. "At least it smells like chocolate? How about we fix this mess with shower sex?" I suggest.

"I'm game for shower sex." Jude agrees. He's sitting up with me straddling his thighs. "Think we can salvage the thong?"

"Is it real chocolate or more of that nasty fake ass crap?" I ask, plucking up the discarded packaging to check. The nutrition facts say it's pure milk chocolate, so I figure it's probably fine. I scoot back enough to get my face to his dick. I avoid the body glitter, tonguing at his cock head while I jerk his shaft until he's nice and hard and tasting salty-bitter with pre-cum. Then I continue jacking his shaft as I mouth at his balls. When he squirms too much, I mouth at the base of his cock where the thong that's more of a heart-shaped chocolate cock ring rests. I lick and stroke and tease him, nibbling at the chocolate with trepidation. It's real chocolate, as the box promised. And it's kind of fun to eat it off of Jude's straining dick with him gasping my name and begging for more. I take my time and I'm not sure if he's going to make it to the shower before he comes. I'd take his entire length in my mouth, if not for the ill-advised glitter of doom.

"Theo, god, I'm close, hun," Jude pants as he tugs my hair. I moan at the sharp sensation, hips jerking because I love a little manhandling when I've got a mouth full of cock. But I want his whole dick and that isn't happening until we rinse off the allegedly edible poison, so I relent, pulling off to grin up at him.

"Shower so I can blow you properly?" I offer.

"Hell yes," he agrees. We gather clean clothes. I peek into the hallway before we make a break for it. We both strategically cover up with the choco-glitter smeared sheets for the dash down the hallway, just in case Jen, or my assorted other roommates, or their significant others are lurking in the hallway.

We giggle like schoolboys getting away with something as we shut the door behind us and Jude presses me up against the closed door to kiss me again. I revel in the press of his body against me, the familiar movements of his lips on mine. I'd never realized how nice it is to know a partner like this. To anticipate his movements and read his mood in the way he touches me. I like it. And the easy affection and how the failed experiment with the glitter results in laughter instead of ruining the mood. I didn't mean to blurt out I loved him earlier, but hell if it isn't the truth.

Jude shifts and the sheet we used to cover up with tugs at me, throwing me off balance. We both fall in a laughing heap of soiled sheets.

"Ugh, let's ditch the evidence of the great glitter fail before it smears over everything in here too," Jude suggests, burrowing out of the bedding. I join him and soon we've got the sheet bundled up in the corner, ready for the laundry hamper, and the room is steaming up from the shower. We get under the hot spray and Jude grabs my washcloth to clean the glitter goo that transferred from his skin to mine while we were wrestling off my chest.

This isn't something I've done with other lovers; let them touch me like this. But I trust Jude. He doesn't pause at my faded top surgery scars, or hesitate at my groin, stroking soap over my dick with no hint he finds it lacking. His touch is tender. When he's done washing me, I take the cloth and return the favor. Lavishing attention on every part of his body, as he did for me. Once we're both clean, Jude sinks to his knees and blows me. I tangle my fingers in his hair, holding him in place. Jude licks and sucks me toward a mind blowing climax that has my T-dick pulsing hard against his tongue and leaves me weak at the knees. When he pulls away, I sink down to sit in the tub with him in my arms.

"Give me a minute and I can return the favor," I offer breathlessly. Jude snuggles into my arms as the pipes rattle ominously.

"Rain check," Jude mutters, jerking out of my arms and lunging for the water to turn it off before we both get blasted with frigid cold. He gets the water stopped before it dips below lukewarm. We towel off and pull on fresh underwear and shirts to slink back to my room. I strip the mattress of the remaining glitter compromised bedding and replace it with my spare set. Then Jude flops down and pulls out his dick, and I give him a BJ before we both fall asleep in a sated heap. He isn't as rough with me as I usually prefer, but with him, I don't mind a little sweetness in our sex life.

CHAPTER 22

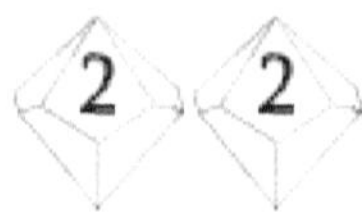

Jude

Theo expected to hear about his surgery date by this week. It's Friday now, and he still hasn't heard from the surgical place. He's been subdued all day. Fretting and antsy all week.

I'm getting worried. What if his claim didn't get approved, or there's some other problem? I know he's worried too. How will he react if his plans fall through? I know how eager he is to get these surgeries. How much he needs them to feel confident in his body.

He hasn't been in the mood for sex for most of the week either. It's possible he's freaked out after our celebration of being together for a month, but I think there's more going on with him. Last night I stayed over at his place, but we didn't do anything more than cuddle and watch a movie in his bed.

This morning, I brushed against his groin while we cuddled and he winced and rolled away from me. That isn't like him at all. He's seemed down ever since, and I have concerns. Theo played it off as no big deal and tried to distract me with a BJ. It came damn close to working, too. My guy knows how to worship a dick, but the way he touched me and looked at me made me think that he wasn't just appreciating my body. There was something desperate and mournful about his touch.

I try not to overthink his mood as we meet up with the gang after work. Pia demanded we all go out tonight, to celebrate her first full week back at the studio. I think she's making up for lost time while she was home with her new baby. Not that I blame them for needing adult time. It just means Theo and I have plans tonight.

Pia can't drink with their new antidepressants. She suggested dancing at a club instead of the gang's usual bar. I'm excited to dance with Theo as a couple.

The entire gang joins us, including Paz and his cousin Alice, Alice's girlfriend and Pia's partner Emil. Their other partner, Gregor, is on baby duty. Even Laura brings a date, much to Max's dismay, since it leaves him and Errol as the only singles in the mix tonight. The others give me the sense that Errol doesn't date or do casual sex.

Theo still seems moody at first, but Gui buys a round of shots for those who are partaking to kick off the festivities. That loosens up Theo. Alice and her girlfriend bicker, as usual.

I end up chatting with Pia, Errol and Emil since we're the only four not drinking. It's nice to get to know Pia and Emil a little better while our friends get their drink on. Paz buys his cousin several rounds after her girlfriend leaves in a huff. Not long after that, Laura's date takes off too, leaving Laura and Alice to commiserate over their shitty love lives.

Several shots after that, Theo is loudly proclaiming how much he loves all of us. He hangs on my shoulders, kissing up my neck, grinding against my ass as he whisper-shouts the wicked things he wants to do to me.

"You know, just because you're pretending to whisper, doesn't mean we can't all hear you, Thee," Pia teases him. Theo flips them the bird, but he stops waxing poetic about my ass.

"Dance with me," he demands, and then he drags me toward the dance floor. I go along willingly. Pia, Emil and Errol finish their soda and join us. Soon the rest of the group is all around us, moving to the music, and it's fun. Not quite the sex-charged grinding from the first few times I went out with Theo, but still fun. Not that he's shy about grinding against me, just less focused on making this into extended foreplay and more fooling around and goofing with our friends.

I'm okay with being a little more circumspect, since my brother is there too, dancing with Paz pressed close to his body for most of the night. Seeing him sappy in love makes me glad of Theo's arms around me during a slower song. We all stay until last call, and then everyone says drunken goodbyes.

Alice wasn't the only one to leave without her date tonight, Errol ushers a very drunk and newly single again Laura out to his car. Emil and Pia are riding with him too. They help guide the stumbling Laura, and slightly less inebriated Max back to the lot where Errol's car is parked.

Alice leaves with Gui and Paz to catch a night bus back to my place. After the fight with her girlfriend, I offered Alice my bed for the night, since I'm not planning to use it. She lives in the burbs and didn't want to drive or deal with a long bus ride home in the middle of the night.

That just leaves Theo and I to walk back to his place. Something changes with his demeanor between saying goodbye to everyone in the press of the crowded club and reaching the sidewalk. It seems too quiet out here, away from the pulsing beat of the music. And he seems quiet too. Restrained and not at all himself. I pretend not to notice, slinging an arm around him when his gait wavers in a drunken stumble. I escort Theo home with a one-sided chat about work and our friends. We tumble into his bed to sleep with nothing more than a chaste goodnight kiss.

CHAPTER 23

Theo

Jude kisses my neck, his morning wood pressed against my ass. I lie there, trying to drum up enthusiasm I can't feel right now. I hate that I'm like this. If Jude was one of my usual tricks, I'd have kicked him out after giving him a BJ last night. Not that I even mustered enough enthusiasm to give him that much before zonking out.

He's not some random trick, though. He matters. I know he's noticed how fucked my head is this past week.

"I love you," he murmurs against my nape.

"Mm," I reply into the pillow. "Tired." We got home late last night, so it's a reasonable excuse. Pia wanted to celebrate her first week back at work with the gang by going out dancing instead of drinking at our usual bar. She said her new meds didn't mix well with booze, but she's always loved to dance. They seem happier this week than they've been since they went on leave.

Jude and I stayed until last call, grinding and teasing each other. The night with my friends lifted my spirits, distracted me from angsting about hearing about my surgery dates, or not hearing. It was fun. Until it wasn't.

Some drunk guy groped me as we were leaving, and it just flipped a switch in my head. He squeezed my packer and leered at me as he mumbled something about big dick energy. I was pretty sure he had no clue the dick in his hand was a prosthetic, but I didn't have the luxury of forgetting that fact.

The thoughts kept racing through my head. Broken. Wrong. Fucked in the head. Never going to be okay.

I roll onto my belly, hands pressed to my head, like I can force out the negative thoughts racing through my mind. There's relief in my flat chest pressed against the sheets. A euphoria in the rightness of my pecs now. It's not enough to obliterate the wrongness I feel about what's between my legs. The sheets rustle as Jude moves away to give me space.

"Do you want me to stay or go?" he asks.

I don't know. He'll have a shitty day if he stays here with me. I shrug, making a noncommittal noise he can interpret however he wants. Jude rests a gentle hand near my shoulder.

"If you want company, I can sit with you and internet on my phone. But if you need space, I'll go," he offers. "Whatever you want, love."

"Stay," I say, groping for his hand. He squeezes my fingers.

"Okay," he says. "Okay, I need to test my sugar and eat breakfast, can I bring you some food?"

"Nah," I say. "Not hungry."

"Okay. I'll be back after I eat. Let me know if you need

anything."

"Uh, huh," I agree.

I drift off into a fitful sleep, dozing away the day. Jude is sitting beside me every time I wake up from napping. True to his word, he just sits with me, not demanding or fussing. Just being there.

It's a comfort when I muster up the energy to roll onto my back and stare at the cracks in my ceiling. My mind is still sleep-fuzzy, and I want to crawl my way back into that blessed unconsciousness. Just forget. Asleep means not having to face my issues. My bladder is having none of that plan.

With a reluctant groan, I scoot my body toward the edge of the bed. Jude gives me a strange look.

"Huh, here I thought no one actually moved like the grinch in the original movie."

"Funny man," I say. I don't have the energy to muster up a genuine smile, and his amusement fading from his face is like a gut punch. I did that. My shitty attitude is going to drag him down and suck all the verve and joy out of him, and I can't stand that thought.

I roll to my feet and trudge to the bathroom to piss. When I retreat to my blanket lair, Jude is waiting for me, a concerned look on his face.

"Are you hungover or sick?" he frets.

"No," I pull the blankets over my head so I won't have to see his earnest face.

"Depressed?" Jude presses.

"Yeah," I acknowledge on a resigned sigh.

"Do you need anything? I can get you water or something to eat?" he offers.

"I'm fine," I roll so my back is to him and curl up in a tight ball, his concern scrapes me raw.

"You're not. But that's okay. Can I hold you?"

I should tell him to go, not drag him into my foul mood. Instead, I nod against my pillow, just a quick gesture. Jude's arms wrap around me and he spoons me until I fall asleep with him holding me tight.

The next time I wake up, he makes me drink some water and eat a few crackers. I don't get out of bed again that weekend, except for the bathroom. Jude stays by my side. A patient presence. I convince him to go home Sunday night.

Monday morning, I consider calling in to work, but I've worried Jude enough. The slew of missed messages on my phone show he's concerned, so I text him back that I'll see him at work, and drag myself to the shower and into the studio.

I'm not very productive, but getting back to my routine occupies my mind and lifts my funk some. A bit before lunch, I get the call I'd been expecting last week. My heart threatens to explode at the name and Montreal area code flashing on my screen. Oh, god, what if they're calling to say they changed their minds? I'm not a candidate for surgery. The province denied my coverage request. I did something wrong with the paperwork, or my therapist's letters didn't agree I need this. Or… I answer with my heart in my throat.

"Hello?" I croak into the receiver.

"Bonjour, j'appelle de la clinique de Montréal. Je peux parler avec Théo Thompson?"

"Um, about my surgery? Yes, this is Theo. *Anglais, s'il vous plaît?*" I reply, the French throwing me off my stride even more than the nerves thrumming through my body. I took French in school, but I'm nowhere near fluent enough to be discussing medical issues in the language.

"Hello, Theo. I'm calling to give you the dates for your surgery," the receptionist replies, switching to English. And just like that, I'm floating on a cloud of euphoria.

It's happening. It's *finally* happening. I fumble through the rest of the conversation, mind reeling that this is real, and I've got so much to do before my surgical date. And I've *got* a surgical date.

I hold back a triumphant whoop. Even I know better than that. My workstation neighbors are already giving me the stink-eye for the loud phone conversation as I confirm my demographic information. I babble out a dozen excited questions about when I need to be in the city, and for how long, and whether I can bring someone to help me. Until recently, that someone was going to be my mom. But now... I find myself asking if my boyfriend can stay with me while I'm recuperating at their post-op convalescent facilities.

As I work out the details, it's strange to feel the bleak cloud of depression lift like a curtain, but I've been here before. I know it's still there. Still lurking in my mind, but for right now, I can't feel anything but jubilant that the surgery I need to feel complete is imminent.

I shouldn't bother Jude while he's working, but he's just upstairs and I am going to explode if I don't share this thrilled happiness with someone. With him. Besides, it's not too early to take a lunch break. I save out of my work and bound up the stairs like an overeager kid on Christmas morning. Jude sits hunched in front of his computer, looking adorably focused when I pounce on him from behind. He startles, letting out a surprised squawk when I wrap my arms around his shoulders and kiss his cheek.

"Oh, fuck, Theo, it's you. You scared me. Is everything okay?" Jude searches my face, his concern evident.

"Everything is wonderful," I assure him. That only deepens his worried frown. I know it's because of how I was acting all weekend. I step back to give him breathing room. Better explain my sudden 180. "I have my surgery date," I exclaim, with a broad grin.

"No shit?" Jude launches himself against me, hugging me tight and rocking me from side-to-side. "They called?"

"Yeah, guess I was just borrowing trouble, thinking there was a problem with the scheduling." I say sheepishly.

"When? Wait, you know what? I've got a million questions. Want to discuss details over lunch?" Jude suggests.

"Next month and discussing it over lunch sounds perfect," I agree.

"Let me just wrap up here." Jude plops back into his office chair and saves out of his work. He shoots off a couple of messages to coworkers. While he's wrapping up, Gui comes over, having noticed my conversation with his brother. He arches a brow as he approaches us.

"What's up, Theo?" Gui asks.

"Got my surgery date, contingent on my bloodwork coming back alright," I reply, attempting to keep my voice down. The whole studio doesn't need to know about my medical stuff, even if I'm thrilled enough to shout it from the rooftops. I beam at Gui and he slaps me on the back in congratulations.

"That's awesome news, man. Congrats. Are you two going out to celebrate?" Gui looks between Jude and I.

"That's the plan, want to tag along?" I offer.

Gui gives Jude a questioning glance before he answers.

"Yeah, come with us. We should celebrate Theo's news," Jude says. I could hug him for not being a territorial boyfriend about this. I want to gush to my bestie and my boyfriend about my good news. Boyfriend. The thought pulls me up short when I realize that's who Jude is to me. The label isn't so scary when the only person I can picture in that role is the sweet guy smiling at me as he logs out of his workstation.

"Ready?" Gui asks.

"I'm good here, should we message the rest of our group chat about joining us?" Jude offers.

"Nah, let's go. I'll tell everyone else on the group chat later. For now, I want to celebrate with my two best guys," I say. I know everyone else will be excited for me. But Gui and Jude are the two I'm closest with. I'm more comfortable sharing the intimate details of my surgery with them. Not to mention my nerves about potential risks versus the thrill of being so close to having everything I've wanted for so long. There's so much work to prepare. Supplies to purchase, bloodwork to complete. I sling an arm around both of them as we walk to the stairs. Jude snuggles into my embrace. Gui gives me a playful shove, so I release him after a moment.

"Thanks for being so supportive," I tell them, meaning it with every fiber of my being.

"Duh." Gui bumps shoulders with me again. "That's what friends are for, right?"

"You'd do the same for us," Jude adds.

I ruffle his hair. "Only because I love you," I tease him. Jude beams, Gui looks a little surprised I said the words. It's getting easier the more I say it.

We're about halfway to the restaurant when I realize I left my wallet in my bag at my workstation.

"If I didn't know you, I'd think you just do this to get me to treat you," Gui jokes with a snort.

"I've got you covered," Jude offers to pay. "Why is your wallet in your bag to begin with, though?"

"It fell out of my pocket and I didn't want to lose it. These pants don't have the most secure pockets," I say, sheepishly. I barely had the energy to drag my ass out of bed this morning, so I wore loose sweats. No duh that they aren't the most secure. Jude eyes my outfit, appreciating how the loose material hangs off my hips. He has to realize that I wore lounge wear to work because I was an emotional mess this morning.

"You feeling better?" he asks, confirming my suspicions that he sees right through me. Gui gives me a concerned look too, but he doesn't comment.

"I am now. Good news perks a guy right up," I say. It's the truth. My funk has lifted for now. Not to say it won't come back, it does that every so often, but for now, with everything I didn't dare hope for within my grasp, I feel fine.

CHAPTER 24

Jude

Once Theo gets his surgery date, things move fast. With the deadline for Battle Fox looming, the timing could be better, but I get the week off to travel with him to Montreal for the surgery. Before I know it, I'm sitting at his bedside in Montreal, fretting over when he's going to wake up from the anesthesia. It's strange to be the one sitting vigil at a medical facility. Stranger still that waiting beside his hospital bed is a positive thing.

Theo was a ball of excited nerves until we got here. The night before the surgery he was quiet, well, quiet for him. Thrumming with anxious nerves. I did my best to distract him from everything that might go wrong in between all the surgical prep he had to take care of the night before. They gave him a pamphlet with instructions about how to clean himself and hair removal at the surgical sites, and it was all a little daunting. We watched a movie with way more explosions that I would normally choose, and he snuggled into my arms in our hotel bed.

For the rest of our stay, he'll be at the hospital or the convalescent center associated with the surgical practice. I'm staying at the hotel, since they restrict visiting hours. The nurses we spoke to earlier were encouraging about Theo having someone there to learn all the wound care stuff with him. There's an extensive list of wound care instructions and symptoms of complications to look out for as he heals.

Then, if all goes well, in ten days we'll fly back to Vancouver for the rest of his recovery. The doc warned Theo many people had a drop in their mood during their recovery after the procedure. It wouldn't suddenly make him a different person or solve all his problems. He knew that, and he assured me he'd be fine. Warned me he'd gotten depressed for a bit after top surgery. Euphoric from the results, but down from the pain and the lengthy healing process.

We know to expect a similar mood drop post-op here, too. I just hope there aren't any serious complications to contend with in the coming weeks. The list of things that can go wrong when Theo was signing the informed consent paperwork was scary.

Theo blinks awake, groggy and disconcerted in his hospital bed. He takes a moment to focus bleary eyes on my face.

"My Jude," he mumbles, reaching toward my face with his dominant hand, then wincing when the motion hurts as he stretches too far. "Ow," he whines. "Why's it hurt?"

"Hush, Thee, you just came out of surgery, remember?"

"No." He frowns, then grips the thin hospital sheet covering his body and lifts it to peek down at himself.

"Did it work?"

His frown deepens.

A nurse pokes into the room. He must have heard us talking. "Look who's awake again, how are you feeling, Theo?" the nurse asks in a bright friendly voice.

"Sore. Can I see the results yet?" Theo asks.

"You asked in the recovery room, too. Your wounds are all bandaged for now. It's best to let things heal between dressing changes. Doc warned you that things might appear a little alarming while you're healing, right? The results you see when we remove the bandages aren't how everything will look in a few weeks. Or months, or years, okay?"

"Yeah. Still want to see my dick," Theo grumbles, but as he says the last few words a broad smile overtakes his expression, and he seems more lucid. "I have a dick now, right?"

"You do." The nurse confirms, sounding bemused, even though he must be used to the patients here being excited about their results. "The procedure went well. Your doctor will be in to discuss everything with you once you're more awake. I'm just going to take a quick peek at your vitals. Then if your pain is bad we can get you a dose of your meds, and let you rest, okay?"

"Okay." Theo agrees. I take his unbandaged hand, his other arm is off limits for now. I squeeze his hand and he squeezes back, grinning at me like a kid who just got the best present ever. How I love that smile.

The nurse bustles around taking readings. A doctor comes and talks to us about the surgery. Theo asks several drug-hazy questions. He's still loopy from the anesthesia. When the nurse changes his dressings, I see the wounds under the bandages at the graft site on Theo's arm. I think it's good he's so out of it, judging from what I can see. They didn't have any major issues, but it was still a major surgery.

Theo got the procedures he wanted. Closure of his front hole, phalloplasty with urethral lengthening, including glansplasty, and the first stage of scrotoplasty. The surgeon explained at the pre-op appointment that in some patients he can connect the urethra during stage one. For others, it has to wait until a separate surgery in another six months. Theo grins when the doctor confirms he'd been able to complete the hookup during the initial surgery.

That means Theo will only need one more surgery in about a year for testicular implants and to insert an erectile device. Technically, he could do it in two procedures. It would mean getting the testicular implant in six months and the erectile device six months later. Between travel costs and time off work to heal, waiting to do both together makes more sense for him.

For now, we're focused on making sure he heals well. They keep him in the hospital for the first three days, and he's encouraged to walk around a few times a day, but otherwise bedbound. The nurses make sure he learns how to care for his wounds, and I learn too, so I can help him when we return home. The week of recovery at the adjacent nursing care facility flies past.

Theo only has a minor issue with some bleeding along the suture lines. And then we're sent home with a stack of papers, reminding us about wound care and potential complications to watch out for. He also gets prescriptions for more pain meds and to get his catheter and sutures removed in two more weeks, a referral for physical therapy for his hand, and an appointment for a telephone follow-up in a month. It's a ton to keep track of, but I'm determined to help Theo get through the next several weeks of healing.

CHAPTER 25

Jude

"This isn't working," Theo proclaims as I open his bedroom door on Saturday around noon. We're a week into his recovery at home. Just over two weeks post-op, and I've been here first thing every day to make sure he's comfortable and has everything he needs. It means skipping my morning workouts, but it's only for the next couple of weeks until he gets his catheter out and can be more mobile. We ate breakfast together this morning, and I only left long enough to grab lunch for us both. But suddenly things aren't working for him?

My heart plummets to my toes at that sickening declaration. "What?" I ask, huh, my voice doesn't even wobble, weird considering how my stomach is churning at his words.

Theo must see my heartache written on my face. He shakes his head vehemently and waves his right arm, wincing when the exaggerated motion pulls on his recovering surgical scars. "No! Not us. I meant this." He waves his hand around his cramped room.

"My mom offered to come take me home for a few weeks while I'm recovering. I don't want you running yourself ragged between work and trying to play nursemaid. I know how important it is for you to maintain your schedule with meals and exercise and stuff. If you make yourself sick trying to take care of me I'll be pissed, okay? And Pia has Emil carting their kid over here to check on me when you can't get away from work, and I don't want to be some giant burden. So, I just meant being laid up in this tiny little room isn't working. You and I are still good, right?"

"Yeah. Of course. We're good. I'll miss you if you go, though. You could still move in with me and Gui. Paz's early shifts mean he's home most afternoons, so you'd have someone to check on you and stuff," I offer, not for the first time. Theo gets the same frozen in fear expression he showed me the last time I made this offer. So I amend it to, "temporarily, just until you feel better."

Theo relaxes at that. "I'm just not ready, Jude. Sorry. It's too big a step right now."

"Okay," I say. I hadn't expected his answer to be any different, but the rejection still stings.

I don't get why he's so resistant to me helping him. We've spent every weekend night together since we started dating. More than a few work nights too. That's on hold now that the surgery makes it inadvisable for him to share a bed. I don't want to jostle him in my sleep, so I already miss that aspect of our intimacy. From that perspective, I guess moving him into my bed won't work well. I can take the couch, though, if it means keeping him close.

"Okay. So. If you want to help me pack? Mom's coming to get me later today."

"Today? When did you plan all this?" I want to ask why he didn't tell me. Why we didn't discuss it before he decided to just fuck off to his hometown between Squamish and Whistler without me. He's pulling away. Is that what this is? Is he running away like he said he might?

"She's been calling every day fussing over me. I gave in last night, and I didn't want to bug you about it over breakfast," Theo answers.

"It's not bugging me to tell me what's going on with you, Theo," I snap.

He raises his hand in defense. "You know what I mean, Jude. I just..." Theo shakes his head and won't meet my gaze.

"You're not a burden," I say through gritted teeth. He's been harping about how hard it must be to be around him or take care of him, and I've had it with his assumptions he isn't worth my effort. I wish he'd believe me. My plan was to just stick around like a nasty rash until he got the point. That won't work with him a two-hour drive away.

"Okay." Theo says dubiously.

"You're not." I blow out a frustrated breath. "Fine, I'll help you get packed. Do I at least get to meet your mom?"

"Oh, uh, sure? I guess? It won't be weird? I haven't ever introduced her to a boyfriend. She already knew Craig, so there wasn't a whole 'meet the parents' thing," Theo seems taken aback by my request. I decide to take it as a good sign that he doesn't object.

"It doesn't have to be weird. I care about you, Theo. I want to meet the important people in your life."

"Does that mean I have to come out to Cali with you to meet your folks? Gui says his Abuela throws the best parties with your whole extended family."

"Yeah, the entire family gets together for cookouts in the summer. Maybe next year or between projects. I kind of blew through my PTO."

"Oh." Theo wilts. "Shit. Does that mean you won't get to see your family for a year because of me? Fuck, Jude, I'm sorry."

I wave him off. "Aunt Mere and Tio Carlo are coming to visit Gui and I at some point this year. Whenever they both get time off work. Now that both their kids are up in Canada, they got their passports so they can make the trip. Gui was teasing them about me being the favorite since he's been up here five years and they finally got the paperwork in after I moved."

"That is compelling evidence," Theo muses. I roll my eyes.

"They worry about me. All of them do." I shrug it off, I'm used to my family babying me a bit. Comes with being the youngest, having a chronic illness, and losing my folks. I guess it ingrained the habit of fussing over me more than Gui. "Doesn't mean they love Gui any less."

"Fair point," Theo says. We sit in awkward silence for a beat.

"Are you running away from me, Theo?" I ask.

"What?" Theo sounds horrified at the idea, and that, more than anything, eases my mind. "No! I just want to be comfortable while I'm convalescing. It'll be nice to have my mom's cooking and snuggle with the family dog while I'm laid up. Bowser is the best at cuddles." Theo gets a goofy grin when he talks about his folks' dog. His expression turns sly, and he adds, "well, he might be my second favorite snuggle buddy now."

"Huzzah, I've dethroned the dog?" I joke.

"Never said *you* were my new favorite. I might just like this new body pillow you got me. A lot." Theo does his goofy eyebrow thing that I think he means to be lascivious, but looks more lovable dork than anything. He pointedly fluffs the pillow I got him to help prop himself up in bed when he complained about being stuck there.

I snort out a laugh. "Sure, if that's how you want to play it, enjoy those pillow snuggles in your cold, lonely bed." I stand to try getting into his closet without disturbing him too much. There's not enough space to maneuver around the mattress without climbing over. The bed squeaks when I rest a knee on it to scoot around the corner.

"Okay, okay," Theo relents. "You're my new favorite, Jude. I've missed waking up with you. It's going to suck, missing you while I'm gone. I, you know, love you and stuff."

"And stuff, huh?" I tease.

"Yeah. All the stuff. With you, okay?" Theo asks.

"Okay," I agree. "So, is your suitcase in here somewhere?" I ask, giving up on looking through the tangle of stuff in the bottom of his closet. I know he has one, since he used it for our trip to Montreal.

"Should be under the bed, yeah," Theo says.

I contort around to check. "This place really is too small," I grumble as I tug the suitcase out from its spot wedged between a couple of plastic totes.

"I know. But the location is perfect, and the price fits my budget." Theo says. The mulish set to his jaw tells me I will not convince him to move no matter what I say next. That's okay. When he's ready, we can find a place together. I can have patience.

There is hardly enough space to free the suitcase. I set it on top of the mattress by Theo's feet and unzip it. His dirty clothes from our trip to Montreal are still packed inside, and we both grimace.

"Oops, guess I should have dumped that in the hamper, sorry."

I sigh. "Next time you could try asking for help, Theo."

"I didn't want to—" he starts to make his excuses, but I've had enough of that BS for one day.

"For the last time, Theo! You. Are. Not. A. Burden," I growl at him.

He grins at me, sheepish, but amused. "Okay then. Tell me how you really feel."

"I love you. We all need help sometimes, Theo. If I needed help, would you think I was a burden? Cause I've got to tell you, I might, like when I have a hypo or if I get sick, I have to take extra precautions. Will you think I'm a burden when that happens? Too much work; time to fuck off and leave Jude to deal with his own shit?" I demand, glowering at him over the pile of dirty laundry.

Theo looks horrified at the idea. "No! Of course not. I wouldn't do that. If you needed me, I'd do everything I could to help you."

"Well, then accept that I feel the same way about you," I say, my tone brooking no argument. I dump the dirty clothing in his hamper and leave his travel sized toiletries packed.

"Sure, I can work on that. I never meant to upset you," he says, all contrition.

"It's fine," I say, hoping he might finally internalize that it's okay to need my help. "Now. Tell me what you want me to pack in here so we can get you ready for your mom."

CHAPTER 26

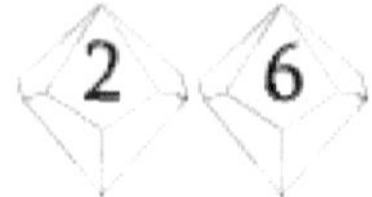

Theo

I knew Jude would argue about my plan to go home for a few weeks. Hence waiting until the last second to tell him. He's been running himself ragged coming over multiple times a day to make sure I have everything I need ever since our return from Montreal. When he can't make it, he's enlisted our friends to check up on me, too. Which, considering I've got my new dick propped up to encourage air circulation and promote healing, is super awkward. I'm proud of my new dick and all, but that doesn't mean everyone I'm close to needs to see it sticking up like I've got a boner as it heals.

It makes me antsy, knowing Jude is going out of his way for me and I can't do much to repay him. We can't even have sex of any sort for at least another month, depending on how fast I heal. Longer, if I develop complications. Other than exploring my new dick solo to stimulate the nerves, it will be weeks until I'm cleared for sex, and longer for anal.

Not that our relationship means I owe him sex. Jude has been pretty clear he doesn't expect that. It's just hard to get past that mindset. The guys I've screwed since Craig only ever stick around long enough to get off and get gone. That's all I've allowed myself. No strings sex and no romantic entanglements means no getting hurt.

Jude has a power to hurt me I haven't given to anyone since Craig. It makes my chest ache to know that I've given Jude my heart to hold. Even knowing he'll take good care of it.

I wish it was easy to tell him as much. The same way he reminds me of his love daily. I don't have that kind of courage. To be so open to letting another person know they're my world.

Mom watches my nephew for my sister on Saturday mornings, so by the time she gets to my place, it's around dinnertime. Jude and I have already eaten and finished packing. She hates driving on the mountain highways after dark, even when the weather is nice like today. I can tell she's eager to get back on the road when she calls to tell me she's parked out front.

Jude helps me out of bed and to the front door, leaving me there to go back for my bag of crap. Too bad I've only got a carry-on sized suitcase. The amount of stuff he seems to think I need for a couple weeks requires a bag of holding or something. He's pretty good at packing, though. All the stuff he'd laid out on my bed seems to fit between my work bag and my suitcase.

I let Mom into the apartment when she knocks. Jude lingers in my room, making sure I'm not forgetting anything I'll miss. I wonder if he's nervous to meet Mom, and that's why he's taking so long.

"There's my baby boy, how are you, Theo?" Mom envelops me in a warm hug that smells like her favorite perfume and reminds me of being a child. That visceral sense memory that these arms will always mean safety.

"Pretty good. Jude's been making sure I stay on top of my pain meds," I reply, making no move to pull free of her embrace.

She rocks me side to side, mindful of my bandaged parts, then holds me at arm's length with a concerned frown. "You're not taking too much, are you?"

"Just OTC meds now," I assure her. "The other stuff left me too loopy to function, and I'm getting enough relief with the Tylenol, if I stay on my schedule. Jude set up reminders in my phone for me." It's not entirely true. I am in a fair amount of pain and I cannot wait to get the irritating catheter removed in a few days, but it's worth it. And the pain is a constant buzzing reminder that I'm whole in a way I've never felt before.

Mom gives me that knowing parent look, "Jude, huh? You know, every time I call the past few months all you say is Jude this and Jude that. Do I get to meet the famous Jude?"

"Yeah, if you promise not to embarrass me," I agree.

"I make no such promises. I've got entire albums of baby pictures I'm just dying to break out and share. There's toddler Theo covered in spaghetti sauce. Preschool Theo dressed up as a monster for Halloween and devouring enough chocolate to keep him wired for an entire week. And don't forget DIY haircut Theo, getting into your father's clippers and shaving yourself bald the day before school photos."

"I was going for a buzz-cut like Craig's," I grumble.

"And if you'd asked instead of assuming we'd tell you

no, you'd have had a buzz-cut instead of being hairless for your grade three photos," Mom reminds me. This whole walk down memory lane is familiar ground; we've recited the story more than once. I love that she sticks to the stories that don't make me dysphoric about who I was as a child.

"It worked out, though," I repeat my familiar line of the story. "That was the year Annie needed chemo. She didn't have to be the only one in our class with no hair. Plus, everyone was used to seeing a bald kid, so she didn't get as much attention over it."

Jude comes down the hall with my suitcase, my work backpack, and a plastic bag.

"You forgot your T and your Switch and your charging cables for your phone and laptop, so I stuffed them in here," he says as he comes around the corner.

"You must be Jude," Mom greets him with a massive grin.

Jude glances up at her, startled. "Yeah, that's me."

"This is my mom, Cathy," I introduce them. Mom's already striding over to give him a hug. "Mom, this is Jude, my boyfriend."

Jude beams like I just gave him a puppy when I call him my boyfriend.

"It's wonderful to meet you, Jude," Mom says. "My son is rather smitten with you."

"Who even says smitten anymore, Mom?" I complain, flushing at the acknowledgement of mushy emotional stuff.

"I do. Now shush and let me get to know your Jude. Tell me about yourself, sweety." Mom releases Jude from her crushing embrace and takes my backpack from him, wrapping one arm around his shoulders to keep him close.

"Um. I work with Theo at Eye-On. I think you know my brother, Gui?"

"Guillermo's visited my house a few times, yes. We missed having him over the holidays this year. How is he?" Mom asks, not batting an eye that Jude and Gui only share a passing family resemblance. They have the same laughing dark eyes. I could kiss her for not making him get into the details of his family life just now.

"He's good. All loved up with his new boyfriend."

"Theo mentioned that. Pascal, right? I hear he makes the world's best brownies. That is high praise coming from my little chocoholic." Mom guides Jude toward the door as they chatter. She pinches my cheek as she calls me a chocoholic. I swat at her hand.

"Mom!" I whine. "I'm not a little kid."

"I realize that, but you'll never outgrow your love of sweets," she says, utterly unapologetic.

"She's got a point," Jude takes her side, the traitor.

"We used to joke he has a separate chocolate stomach, so even if he stuffs his regular stomach full, he can still eat his chocolate. I swear he could sniff the stuff from a mile away, I never found a hiding spot he couldn't ferret out."

"Chocolate is meant to be enjoyed, not hidden," I inform them with a haughty sniff. "Why are we talking about things I can't have while I'm healing?" I add with a pout. All sources of caffeine, including chocolate, are off limits for a few more weeks. When I move to cross my arms over my chest, it hurts the healing donor site on my left arm. Ouch. I'm unsure whether to be happy Mom and Jude are getting along or miffed that they're teasing me. I'm leaning toward happiness. Jude fitting in with my family makes me smile. If I let myself go there, I want him to be part of my family. Someday. In the future. The distant future. No jumping the gun and ruining things.

"I thought you wanted to get back on the road, Mom," I remind her, reaching for my suitcase.

She snatches it out of my grasp. "Nuh uh, you're not doing any lifting until you recover. You sit and let Jude and I get your things in the car. Then we'll help you down the walkway."

"I can walk on my own," I complain.

"Of course you can, dear, but humor your mother and let us help you. Stubborn boy, just like your father."

"And my mother," I grumble

"Well, yes. You got a double dose of the stubborn streak," she agrees. "Now, put on your shoes, Theo."

I hobble to a kitchen chair with my shoes and work on the laces while Mom and Jude take my things to the car. I'm sure they're talking about me, but I don't mind. It's nice. Two people I love getting acquainted, acting like they see a future where they're close.

By the time I get my shoes onto my feet, I'm in agony from bending and stretching to reach. I might be overdoing it a little. That's a depressing thought. All I did was walk down the hall and pull on my shoes.

Jude comes back without my mom. "Hey, you okay?" he asks.

"Sore," I reply, no sense lying to him.

"Let me help?" He asks. I nod, no sense hurting myself for the sake of my pride.

He clucks over me as he does up my laces and helps me to my feet.

"Get well fast, no overdoing it. I'll try to convince Gui to visit you for a weekend. Is that overstepping?" Jude fusses.

"I'd like that," I say. It's the truth. I'll miss Jude's goofy grins and waking up with him wrapped around me. His morning wood poking into my hip. And it hits me that the next time we get to wake up together, my actual flesh and blood dick will poke into him for once. It might not be quite cis, but it's there now. Real and warm. I can imagine how it will feel between our bodies. I beam at him.

"What's the giant smile for?" Jude asks.

"Just thinking about waking up with you," I say. That's the important part. That it's him in my mundane little fantasy.

"Mm, that is something to smile about. As soon as you're recovered enough. Okay? I love waking up with you," Jude says. He leans up to kiss my cheek. I pull him into a proper kiss in the doorway. Jude clings to me, careful of my surgical sites even as his tongue explores my mouth. He kisses me like he wants to memorize my taste of my lips against his. We only break apart when my mom clears her throat from the doorway.

"You ready, Thee? I don't want to rush you, but you know I prefer to avoid driving in the dark," she says.

"Ready," I agree.

"Don't forget your phone," Jude grabs it from the floor where I set it to deal with my shoes, and hands it over to me. "You stay in touch, right?"

"Don't worry, I'll message you so much you'll be sick of me before you can even miss me." I wink at him.

He shoves my shoulder gently. "That will never happen. No running away, promise?"

"I promise. Call you tonight."

"I love you, Theo. It was nice to meet you, Cathy."

"Lovely to meet you too, Jude. Like I said, you and

your brother are welcome to visit anytime." Mom pats Jude's arm, the same sort of familiar caresses she gives me and my siblings.

"Love you too, Jude," I mumble, giving him a chaste peck on the lips before Mom takes my arm and guides me out the door. It's embarrassing how much I need the help to hobble down the single step to the walkway and to climb into the car.

Jude remains standing by the door, waving to me as Mom hovers over me, helping with the seat belt before going around to get in the driver's seat.

CHAPTER 27

Theo

I pop a Tylenol from the backpack Jude packed for me before we get more than a block. The car's movements are not fun when everything is still so sore. The first part of the drive passes in silence as I grip the oh shit bar to keep from tensing against every acceleration and curve in the road.

Mom notices my white-knuckled grip and apologizes the entire way. Once we get across the Lion's Gate Bridge and onto the Sea to Sky highway, the ride is much smoother and I can relax. Mom relaxes too, no longer contending with traffic and mom guilt about causing her baby pain.

She pats my thigh, luckily missing the area they used to graft the donor site on my arm. "Sorry about the traffic, dear. I'm glad that part is behind us. How are you doing?" she asks.

"I'm hanging in there," I reply.

"So, you and Jude?" Mom pries.

"Yeah." I sigh, half-exasperated and half-dreamy.

"You're in love with him," Mom says. She knows me too well to even bother pretending that's a question.

"Yeah," I agree.

"But you asked me to take you home so you won't have to move in with him while you're recovering."

"Yeah." I recline my seat as far as it will go to rest.

"Want to explain why?" Mom glances over at me.

"I don't want to scare him off." I fidget with my seatbelt, adjusting the way it lays across my chest.

"Baby, that boy is just as in love with you as you are with him. You won't scare him off with your gross morning breath," Mom assures me.

I pluck at my seat. "Yeah, he doesn't mind my morning breath. It's more the way I get. You know?"

"The way you get?" Mom sounds puzzled before she figures out what I mean and frowns at me. I love that my mom takes it in stride that I just told her I sleep with my boyfriend and doesn't make it into a thing. "You mean your depression?"

"Yeah."

She purses her lips. I know it's killing her not to tell me I should reconsider medication. She's not wrong. Not entirely. But the meds I've tried had side effects that I couldn't cope with. Headaches so intense they left me bedridden. Pain meds didn't touch them. That was the first one I tried.

Then the second one made my head all foggy and the third one killed my libido. At that point, I'd been trying various medications for over a year and I'd gotten on T and had my top surgery scheduled so the depression wasn't as bad.

I still get the occasional days where I can't drown out my negative self-talk. But my depression improved exponentially once I started my transition, so I convinced myself I didn't need the medication. Besides, I didn't want to be messing with a new med while recovering from surgery, so I just never filled the prescription for the fourth medication after my top surgery.

"Have you spoken with him about it?" Mom asks instead of suggesting meds.

"Yes. I told him about Craig," I admit.

"And?" she prompts me.

"And he told me it doesn't change how he feels."

"Oh, well, that is a problem then," Mom says, her tone worried. I blink, startled at her response. She's usually more optimistic.

"It is?" I ask, blinking at her.

Mom nods. "Sure. If he's in the habit of lying to you, I can see why you wouldn't trust him at his word."

I bristle at the implication that Jude is a liar until I realize her intent. I roll my eyes. "Jude isn't a liar," I grumble.

"Then why don't you believe him?" Mom glances over at me, one eyebrow raised in challenge. God, I recognize that look from the mirror. The drive with my mom reminds me just how much I'm like my family. And how much I miss them with my infrequent visits. Much as the next few weeks without Jude will suck, I'm glad of the chance to see my folks and my siblings.

I groan and scrub at my face. "It's complicated."

"Only if you make it that way," Mom replies. She might have a point.

"I think I'm going to take a nap. All this healing takes it out of me." I deflect with a huge fake yawn that becomes a real one half-way through.

"Sweet dreams, sweetie. Think about what I said," Mom says.

I pretend to snore rather than replying. Mom chuckles, reaching over to ruffle my hair instead of calling me out on my avoidance. She flicks on the radio. It doesn't take long for the steady vibrations of the car and the low crooning of her favorite oldies' station to lull me to sleep.

CHAPTER 28

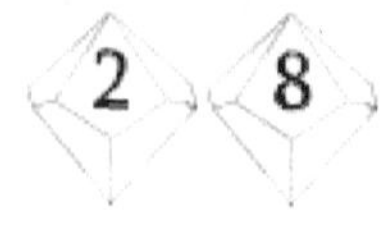

Jude

It's been a week since Theo left for home. At first, he appears jovial about being with his family and his recovery. We chat back and forth throughout the day, every day. Video calls each night help with missing him. He pops in and out of our private chat and our group chat with our friends between napping and hanging out with his family.

On our Friday night call, he even lets me talk to his family before they start a movie night. He introduces me to his older sister, Erin, and brother, Tyler. And Bowser. The family dog is a gray ball of fluff who barks at the phone when Theo baby talks to him.

I have a quick chat with his Mom and Dad, ending with them renewing the invitation to drive out for the weekend while Theo is recuperating. They hand the phone to Tyler, who looks so much like Theo that they could be twins, except Ty's hair is shorter and an undyed light auburn. He's lounging against another man whom he introduces as his husband, Fred. They both seem nice.

"So, you're the first guy to keep this one's attention for more than a hot second, eh?" Ty greets me.

"Guess so," I agree with an awkward shrug.

"Knock it off, Ty," Theo shoves his brother and reaches to take the phone away from him.

"Hey, not my fault you're a notorious player," Ty says defensively as he keeps the phone away from his brother. The spinning camera makes me a bit dizzy, but I can't help smiling at their antics. It's in the same vein as the things Theo's roommates say to him, but coming from his brother there is genuine affection in the ribbing.

"Pass it here. I want to meet the new boyfriend, too," Erin demands. The phone spins to face a smiling woman who shares the same resemblance as Ty and Theo. All three kids take after their mother. Erin waves at the camera. A toddler with flyaway curls sits perched on her lap.

"This is Skyler, my nephew," Theo introduces the kid by reaching over to muss his hair.

"Who dat?" Skyler asks through the thumb in his mouth. His other hand clutches onto his mother's shirt.

"That's Uncle Theo's boyfriend, Jude," Erin replies.

"Unca Jude?" the kid asks, glancing at Theo, who has sidled closer to be in the camera frame with his sister.

Erin bites back a bray of laughter at the question. Theo blanches. I laugh off the pang of longing that innocent question evokes. I want to be part of his family.

"Maybe someday, if I'm lucky, kiddo, for now, just Jude is fine," I say. Theo gives me a grateful look.

"Why?" Skyler's little forehead crinkles in confusion. He takes his thumb out of his mouth to say, "Unca Ty's boyfwend is Unca Fwed." Nothing like toddler logic to give me an emotional kick in the balls.

"Because, Sky, Uncle Fred and Uncle Ty have been together for a long time. Ty and Fred are married. They love each other and Uncle Fred is part of our family," Erin explains patiently. Then she stumbles as she says, "Uncle Theo's only been dating Jude for a little while. Jude isn't —"

"You can call him Uncle Jude," Theo blurts.

"You sure?" Erin and I both ask.

"Yeah," Theo nods. "He's family, too. Call him Uncle Jude, Sky."

"Okay," Skyler shrugs and snuggles into his mother's arms. "Wanna watcha mobie wid us Unca Jude?" Skyler's thumb goes back to his mouth, making his words hard to parse, and his eyes dart up to the television behind the phone. The kid has lost interest in the new person on the video chat now that he knows what to call me.

"I can't tonight. Maybe when I visit in a couple of weeks," I reply.

"We've lost him to the great and powerful screen," Erin laughs. "Nice to virtually meet you. I guess we'll be seeing a lot more of you, Uncle Jude," Erin says, an amused twinkle in her eye.

Theo takes the phone back. "That's okay, right?"

"More than okay," I agree. "I'll let you get to your movie, Thee. Love you."

"Love you. I'll text you later," Theo promises, then he signs off the call.

We text throughout the movie, much to Gui's annoyance since he, Paz, and I are playing a card game with Alice. She and her girlfriend had another fight and broke up again. She swears this time is permanent, so Paz invited her over to cheer her up. That devolves into Alice and Paz drinking and commiserating over her ex's latest hurtful behavior and Alice planning a summer of loving nature instead of girls. She and Paz like to hike, so it makes sense that she'd have more time for her hobbies without the ex who hated to get sweaty.

I retreat to my room where Theo and I fool around on video chat. Now that his catheter is out and the incisions are healing well, he's cleared to touch his new dick. He's not supposed to have sex yet, but stimulating the healing tissue is allowed as long as he stops if anything hurts.

On Saturday, Theo asks me to jerk off for him on camera, so I give him a private show before we join our friends for an online video game night. Gui loads an old copy of Age of Mythology onto my laptop. It takes some trial and error to figure out my old account's password from when we used to play together ages ago.

With the entire group, plus our significant others, we play five versus five over a virtual private network. Theo, Paz, Gui, Pia and I kick Errol, Max, Emil, Gregor, and Laura's butts two times out of three.

It's fun, and I love that we're able to include Theo so he doesn't feel left out. He grumbles about his healing arm slowing him down, but I'm pretty sure he enjoys himself, anyway. The PT person he saw suggested video games as a good exercise for his arm's rehabilitation, so it's a win-win in my book. It's a good night.

Then the texts from Theo get fewer and further between. His mood seems down more each time I get a reply. By the end of the second week staying with his parents, I go from getting multiple replies an hour to one or two texts a day. He only seems to say he's tired and sore and doesn't have the energy for chatting or playing online games or doing a video or voice chat before bed.

When I call his phone on Friday around our usual time, his mom is the one who answers.

"Jude?" Cathy asks when she answers.

My heart catches in my throat as the sickening worry that something happened to him grips me.

"Yeah," I squeak. "Is he okay?"

"Oh, goodness, yes," Cathy assures me, she sounds far too bright to be lying about it. "Of course, dear. I'm sorry to have worried you. Theo's napping. He left his phone downstairs, and I didn't want you to worry about not getting an answer when I saw your name on the caller ID."

"Is he doing alright?" I ask, swallowing around the lump in my throat. He's okay. If my thundering pulse would get that message, that would be great.

"He's a little down. He claims it's just coming down from the surgery and being grumpy about being in pain."

"His surgeon mentioned that," I say, dubious.

Cathy sighs. "You know this isn't unexpected for him, right?"

"Yeah." I say. "I wish he was here so I could keep him company."

There's a pause, and then Cathy sighs. "I think you're good for my son. When he wakes up, I'll let him know you called."

"Thanks. Tell him it's okay if he doesn't have the energy to call me back. Would it be okay if I visit him this weekend? It's not too far of a drive and I have a friend with a car..."

"You are welcome here anytime, Jude. Do you want to surprise Theo or should I let him know to expect you?"

"I don't want to disappoint him if I can't make it after all, so let's plan on keeping it a surprise?"

"That would be lovely. Let me give you my number so

I can text you the address and you can call when you arrive, if Theo isn't answering his phone."

"Thanks, Cathy."

We exchange phone numbers and I end the call. A few minutes later, I get a text from Theo's mom with her home address. Then I text Alice to see if she wants to take a road trip tomorrow. She mentioned wanting to hike Whistler when she visited last weekend. It might be a long shot, but I can't stand not being there for Theo when he's depressed.

CHAPTER 29

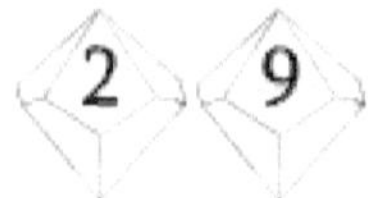

Theo

The only reason I know it's Saturday morning is that Skyler is screaming and banging on pots or something in the kitchen, directly below my bedroom. It's a very loud reminder that Mom watches him for Erin on Saturdays so my sister can have time to run errands.

Erin is a single parent by choice. My asexual aromantic sister wanted a kid with no relationship entanglements, and she is rocking the single mom thing. She used a sperm donor and ART to conceive Skyler. And he's perfect. I just wish her adorable little hellion wasn't making such a racket while I'm trying to sleep.

At some point, I give up burrowing under my pillows to block out the noise and glance at the clock. Ugh. Okay. Noon is hardly an ungodly hour to be awake and making noise. Guess I can't be too mad at the munchkin.

Not that I have the energy to get mad, anyway. Mostly,

I want to shut my eyes and drift back to sleep. My bladder is the only thing stopping me. I'm not so miserable that I'm going to just lie here until I piss myself. And I'm supposed to empty my bladder regularly so as not to put extra pressure on my new dick. Besides, changing the sheets is way more effort than dragging my ass across the hall to the toilet. It still takes me an age of staring at my ceiling to force my muscles to cooperate.

I should go downstairs and eat something. I slept through dinner last night. Mom brought me up a plate, but I pretended not to wake up when she offered it to me. If Jude were here, he'd have brought me breakfast. That thought makes me reach reflexively for my phone on the nightstand where Mom left it when she brought up my food last night. I forgot it in the living room yesterday, when she insisted that I needed to get out of bed and mope in a new location for a while.

Before I can let the voice that says I shouldn't bother Jude with my bullshit take control, I shoot off a text.

Theo: Miss you. Wish I could kiss you.

No reply. I stare at my screen for a few minutes. What do I expect, when I've been ghosting him all week?

It's unreasonable to want him to text me back this instant when I've been a twat to him. I toss the phone aside, rub at my eyes with a loud groan, and roll onto my feet.

I stumble to the washroom and take way too long to get through my entire morning routine. Every tiny task requires a pep talk. Like I can't quite figure out how to sit on the toilet, or how to tackle the monumental task of washing my hands and face. Now that my catheter is out, peeing with a dick is different. The fact everything is healing makes it a bit of a process, anyway. Still, I feel like crap that even using the toilet seems too hard right now. Adulting fail.

When I trudge back into my room, my phone screen is lit up with a new message.

Jude: Miss you too.

I stare at my phone and plop back into my blanket nest, pulling the covers over my head. I want to keep the conversation going, but I can't figure out what else to say. Nothing seems right. The screen turns off. Downstairs, Skyler squeals with glee.

He says something that sounds like, "Hi, Unca!" The kid is as loud as the rest of the family. No surprise there.

Ty must be here. I wonder if Mom enlisted my brother and Fred to drag me out of bed today. She's been trying to get me to come downstairs at least once a day. If nothing else, I'm supposed to walk a few times a day for blood circulation reasons and keep my bladder empty for healing reasons. I should play with my nephew while he's here. I don't see Sky often enough. Too bad I can't quite seem to leave my blanket den. Maybe after a nap.

My phone buzzes before I can drift off to sleep.

Jude: You got room in your blanket fort for two?

Theo: Huh?

Someone knocks on my door.

"Come in," I call, assuming it's Mom coming to check on me.

The door opens, the light tread moving across the floor isn't Mom. I know that footstep. Recognize it from the sounds he makes when he lets me sleep in after a late night. The bed dips when he perches on the edge of the mattress and reaches a tentative hand to stroke the blanket lump I'm hiding under. He pats my hip for a second before working up to my head and resting there.

"Are you really here?" I ask.

"Yeah," Jude says. "Wanted to surprise you."

"I'm surprised," I croak, throat tight with emotion. I missed his steady presence this week.

"Is it a pleasant surprise?" he asks. That intensifies my desire to hide, and I duck out from under his hand. How could he doubt I'd want to see him? Duh, I've acted withdrawn all week. I'm hiding under my blankets like a kid afraid of the dark instead of hugging the stuffing out of him like any normal boyfriend would do after two weeks apart. The better question is how could I let him doubt whether I'd want him here. I don't have an answer. Jude pulls back his hand and I know he's going to get up and leave if I don't reply.

"Good. It's good," I force out the words. I shuffle around enough to lift a corner of the blanket. "Room for two," I mumble.

Jude slips into the covers with me, cuddling into my side, careful of my healing bits.

"I missed you," he murmurs into our quiet little bubble. I wrap my good arm around him.

"Me too." I'm not any better for having him there. I still can't seem to muster up much interest in leaving my bed, let alone doing anything. But I'm not alone in this, and that's nice.

A while later, Mom knocks on my door with a tray of food. The aroma of soup and fresh baked bread makes my stomach gurgle and my mouth water. Jude sits up. I don't snap at him about pulling the covers off my head.

"You're awake, good. Here, I brought you lunch, think

you can eat something?" Mom asks as she sets up the tray on my dresser.

"Thanks, Mrs. Thompson," Jude says.

"Cathy, dear. Let me know if you need anything else." She flashes Jude a fond smile before she leaves.

"I need to grab my bag from downstairs, my test supplies are in it," he says, sliding out of my bed.

"Okay," I mumble.

"Can I get you anything?" he offers.

"I'm good."

Jude goes to get his stuff. With anyone else, I'd be trying to figure out a way to get them to leave. Even Gui grates on my nerves when everything gets to be too much.

Jude is an exception. He doesn't make demands or expect more from me than I can give. He just crawls into my blanket nest with me and hunkers down until the storm passes and I can function again.

By the time Jude returns, my soup has cooled enough to try a few sips. We spend the weekend cuddling. Jude sleeps in my old sleeping bag on my floor, refusing to risk bumping me in his sleep. He talks to me, sharing all the latest work gossip. He doesn't get upset when I just let his voice wash over me without paying attention to the details. Alice picks him up to return to the city on Sunday night, and I promise to do better about staying in touch.

Monday, Jude and I message back and forth a few times and I gather up the energy to watch some streaming shows on my phone. By Tuesday, I'm up to venturing out of my blanket lair. I'm still sore, but my spirits improve steadily.

I get back to messaging my friends daily and we play video games together online in the evenings. Jude and

I video chat daily. My family plans movie nights or we play cards around the kitchen table after dinner. I make the most of my remaining time home to convalescence.

The next several weeks of recovery are physically draining. But, at six weeks post-op, my wounds have healed enough that I can look in the mirror and see a body that matches my self-image. It means the world.

It's like the first time I used a packer, this bubble of perfect happiness. I cried then. And I cry again as I stand nude in front of the mirror in my parent's guest washroom and see someone complete for the first time. Not that I was truly broken before, but this feels so much more right for me and my journey. Sure, the angry red scars remain, marking that I had to fight for this body, but I don't want to hide anymore. No part of me cringes at the person reflected at me. I've never had that before. Glimpses, sure, but never this profound euphoric bliss.

This is like all those little things combined. The moment I first noticed thick dark body hair making my legs look like my ideal vision of a man's. The moment I got my first binder. That first glimpse of my profile with a packer's bulge and a flat chest under my baggy t-shirt and a stranger called me 'sir'. The first time I successfully grew out my facial hair. But this, with my phallo healing, is the first time I can stand completely naked and be at peace with myself.

It's everything. And for once, the bitchy voice at the back of my head telling me lies, remains silent. I don't feel broken or incomplete. I'm just me and I can be enough. For Jude and for myself.

I have a follow-up appointment with my surgeon via

telephone to sign off that I'm healing well. Then I make plans to return to Vancouver and my job on Monday. I'm eager to get back to work and run my game again. Pia ran a couple of Paranoia one-shots while I was away. I spectated via video chat on Jude's phone. It was fun, but I'm itching to get back in the GM seat of our VentureQuest campaign. The gang has a dragon to rescue. And I've got a boyfriend who deserves to know just how much he means to me after he stood by me through the lowest lows of my recovery.

CHAPTER 30

3 0

Jude

Theo has been in much better spirits since my surprise visit to his Mom's house last month. He stuck by his decision to stay with his family until his doctor cleared him to return to work at six weeks post-op. After meeting them all in person, I can see why. It's clear how much his family loves and supports him. That doesn't stop me from missing my boyfriend.

The day he's supposed to come back, I'm a ball of nervous energy. Theo seems more like his usual self since my visit. Bright and happy. When I was there, Theo dragged himself downstairs on Sunday. We watched movies with his nephew and shot the shit over a card game with his siblings. His mom baked for us and his dad quizzed me about my job and my family. I liked them, how could I not when they reminded me so much of Theo?

This morning, Paz and Gui wanted to take me out to distract me, but I was eager not to be a moment late greeting my guy. His mom helped me spirit away his apartment key at my last visit so I can tidy up his stuff before he gets home.

His decision to recover at home had been last-minute enough that he left a hamper full of dirty laundry awaiting his return. Let alone the clothing that never got washed after our stay in Montreal. I don't want to spend his first day back dealing with chores and crap, so I take the initiative to clean his room. It's a bit of a disaster, to be honest. I find a bunch more of his dirty clothes under the bed. His lucky D20 had rolled into a corner. I'm tempted to text him a pic, but then he'll want to know where I found it. That will give away my surprise. A little before I expect him to arrive, I get a text from Theo.

Theo: Groan. Lost my keys. Again. I'm going to text Jen or something. Fingers crossed that I just left them in my room. They're going to kill me if we have to get the locks changed again. Good thing we aren't a reality show house, or I'd get voted out over this.

Jude: Can't we just get a spare cut if you borrow one from Jen or Donna?

Theo: It's a security risk, so they'll want to re-key everything. They thought one of my tricks stole the last one I lost, and they seemed convinced he'd come back and rob us. As if we have anything worth stealing. *eye roll*

Jude: Are you going to text Jen to let you in when you arrive, then?

Theo: Yeah. I'll let you know when I'm inside so you can come over, if you still want to visit tonight?

Jude: Duh. Just try to keep me away ;)

Theo: Can't wait to see you. It's been 4ever.

Jude: More like five evers ;P

Theo: Infinite evers. I've never seen you before in my life. Who even are you?

Jude: Too far.

Theo: Yeah. You are way too far away. Gonna have to fix that.

Jude: Can't wait to see you.

It's only been two weeks since my visit, and we video-chatted last night. Still way too long. A part of me wondered if some distance would dampen the intensity of what I feel for Theo. It hasn't. His absence only makes me want him more.

I wish he'd move in with me, but I promised myself I won't harp on him about moving in with me. My initial offer was about the practicalities of his surgical recovery, but now I just don't want to wake up anywhere other than in his arms. And I low key hate his apartment. The location is great, but his roommates razz him constantly. It isn't quite mean-spirited, but I see the way it gets to him sometimes. His room is a glorified closet. I want better for him.

Jen knocks on Theo's door while I'm putting the freshly laundered sheets back on his bed.

"Knock, knock," she says.

"Come in," I call.

"Hey, Jude." Jen leans on the doorframe to chat since there isn't really room for us both to stand in the narrow strip of floor beside the bed. "Theo just texted me to say he misplaced his keys. Am I correct in assuming you're the culprit? Are you waiting to surprise him?"

"Yeah, hope that's not an issue?" I ask.

"Nah, it's fine. We're totes going to rag on him for letting his guy steal his keys again, though. Better than all the missing shit when he paraded a constant stream of dick through his bed every night," Jen says. She waves away my concern with another casual bit of slut-shaming Theo. It pisses me off, but he still has to live with her, so I bite my tongue.

She must notice my annoyance because she rolls her eyes at me. "No shade, Jude, but your boyfriend was a total fuckboy before you came along." She twirls her hair around her finger as she talks, the epitome of sorry, but not sorry. Like she wants to stir up trouble or get me to agree that Theo's sex life is any of her business. Or even my business. "You have no idea."

"Okay. Thanks. Did you need anything else?" I ask through gritted teeth.

"No, I'm heading out, but I wanted to let you know that I told Theo I'd leave the door unlocked for him when he gets in. Have a nice evening." Jen winks at me and leaves me to finish making the bed and putting away Theo's laundry.

When everything is as clean as it's going to get, I flop onto the clean sheets to wait for Theo's arrival. Jen might be out, but I saw Donna and her boyfriend earlier in the kitchen. Their other two roommates and their significant others are in the living room watching some reality TV marathon. I have no interest in socializing with people who make a sport of tearing my guy down. Jen is the nicest of the lot, and that says something.

I jerk upright at the sound of the apartment door opening and Theo's roommates calling out variations on welcoming him home.

"Hey, glad to be home. I want to get settled in, we can catch up later, or something," Theo brushes them off and his footsteps approach his room. When he opens the door and sees me sitting on the edge of his bed his face lights up.

"Hey, Jude," he says, dropping his backpack in the hallway and launching himself at me, tackling me back onto the bed. Before I can fuss over him taking it easy with his still healing grafts, he takes my face between his hands and kisses me soundly. He straddles me, his groin pressed against my belly, with none of his usual body-shyness about his dick in evidence as our lips lock.

I work my hands into his pants, squeezing his ass and encouraging him to grind his dick into me. Even if he can't get hard without another surgery, he says it still feels good. I'm all for fooling around after almost two months of going without this part of our intimacy. The frantic kissing gives way to something sweeter. A gentler exploration, as we get reacquainted with each other's bodies.

Theo eventually pulls back and grins at me.

"Love you, but we should stop humping. My mom's still in the car with Erin and the rest of my stuff. Did she know you'd be here?" Theo asks. He doesn't climb out of my lap.

"Yeah. She helped me swipe your keys," I admit.

Theo shoves at my chest. "You jerk! I was sure I'd lost them and some serial killer was going to find them and ax murder all my roommates. How would I afford rent here on my own?"

"Glad your priority isn't their lives, it's their share of the rent," I tease him. Theo sticks out his tongue at me.

"I mean, they're jerks, but I don't actually want them to get ax murdered. Even aside from the rent angle. Although, if you brought me welcome home brownies and their deaths mean I don't have to share the baked goods..."

I shove him out of my lap with a chuckle. "Good to know all it takes to get you to sanction murder is Paz's brownies."

"I mean, you saw my surgical care paperwork, right? They have denied me chocolate and any form of caffeine for far too long. It's inhumane," Theo reminds me.

"You poor dear, you're positively wasting away," I say dryly. We kiss again, like neither of us can quite keep our affection to ourselves.

"Hey, Jude?" Theo asks.

"Yeah?" I push his hair off his face.

"Want to take me to your place?" he suggests.

"Why? Do you want to ask Paz for his chocolate?" I tease. He never asks to come over. Probably because Gui lives there and the two of us fucking with my brother in the next room is, less than ideal.

"No." Theo shakes his head. "I want to hang out with you and I don't want to deal with the roomies razzing us."

"You know, there's a simple way to never deal with their shit again," I say, unable to help myself.

"Are you asking me to move in with you, Jude?" Theo bats his lashes at me.

I shrug so as not to come across too pushy, I promised I wouldn't pressure him.

"You realize I'd drive Paz nutty." Theo gestures to his room. "I'm not the tidiest guy."

"He puts up with Gui," I say, excited because that isn't a no. "And my brother is a slob, god love him."

"Yeah, but Gui sleeps with him, it's different. I thought we might get a place. Just the two of us," Theo suggests. The wall behind my head must have become fascinating, judging from the way he's scrutinizing it to avoid looking at my face.

"Yeah?" I ask.

"Yeah. If you want? The past few weeks gave me time to think and I hate not waking up with you. So. What do you say?" He darts his eyes to my face to gauge my reaction.

"I need to give Gui notice, but I'd like that."

"Cool. I have to give the roomies a couple months notice so they can line up someone new to sublet the room. But we can look now, for later this summer."

"In the meantime, you want to stay with me at Paz and Gui's?" I offer.

"Yeah." Theo nods. "That works. If they're okay with it."

"Gui can hardly complain. He lives with his boyfriend, he'd be a hypocrite if he said I can't do the same. Anyway, we should go find your mom and sister so they're not sitting in the car forever."

"Sure, I left most of my stuff in the car. We can head over to yours now. Mom offered to take us out for dinner some place. She and Erin have a hotel booked so they can have a shopping and spa day tomorrow before they head back home. Dad, Fred, and Ty have Skyler out on a weekend fishing trip to like, renew their man card registration or some shit."

"You didn't want in on the manly bonding time?" I ask.

"Nah, they invited me along, but I want to get settled

in before going back to work on Monday and I missed you. Plus, I have never shared their interest in standing around bodies of water and getting eaten by tiny insects. Just so I can catch and eat trout that taste like the mud where they swim. Pretty sure my fishing license expired ages ago, and Bowser smells foul when he gets in the water. That dog loves to swim. Besides, Mom and Erin could use a day of relaxation. Shuttling my ass home was a good excuse for them to have a city getaway. I don't begrudge them their mother-daughter bonding time, either."

"That's fair," I agree. I grab the bag Theo brought inside with him and we leave.

We exchange vague pleasantries with his roommates on our way out of the apartment and much friendlier greetings with Theo's mom and sister when we get to the car. I give his mom directions to my place. She has me text Gui to invite him and Paz out with us.

Theo and his sister squabble over where to get dinner. Theo plays the healing after a major surgery card. Erin argues the single parent's one kid-free night in the city angle. His mom asks for my input, since she knows I have dietary restrictions. We settle on a place I know Theo enjoys that has enough menu options to please everyone. Gui and Paz agree to come along, though Gui puts up a fight over letting Mrs. Thompson pay for all of us. It reminds me of home and the big family dinners I've missed since moving. I can't help a goofy grin at the rightness of having part of Theo's family gathered together with a part of mine.

CHAPTER 31

3 1

Epilogue

Theo

We meant to look for a new place once I told my roomies I was moving in with Jude. As it happens, I enjoy living with Paz and Gui. I get to sleep next to Jude every night, and wake up with him in my arms every morning. Gui and Paz are an upgrade on my old roommates in every sense.

Paz is forever experimenting with baked goods that he lets me mooch off him as long as I contribute to buying the ingredients. That's a bargain I am more than happy to accept. Gui and I can play video games together whenever we want. It's an awesome setup. Sure, more space would be nice. Or a layout where our bedrooms don't share a wall, but I'm not in any hurry to move again now that all my stuff is here. The only downside to living with my boyfriend's brother is that we have to keep the noise down when we fuck.

Since I finally have doctor's clearance to test out my new dick, that's been interesting to work around. So far, I've decided that I love blowjobs and frotting. The visual alone is almost enough to have me close to coming. My dick rubbing alongside Jude's, or disappearing into his mouth, hot as fuck. And jerking myself while Jude fucks me is nice, too.

I haven't topped him yet. It'll be the better part of the year before I can get the surgery to add the erectile device to my dick. Until then, figuring out workarounds to get hard enough for penetration means looking at external erectile devices. I ordered one, once everything healed up enough to take measurements, but that's still in the mail. Too bad, since I'm really looking forward to trying it out, and I have a feeling my plans for today will lead to some epic sexcapades later tonight.

Not that a pesky little detail like not getting my dick inside Jude's ass yet is going to stop us. Technically, Gui might still be here, since his work hours are as flexible and as mine and Jude's. Paz has a shift this morning, though, so Gui probably left for work early, too. That way he can hang with his man for a couple hours between work and our game tonight.

I wake Jude up with kisses, my dick pressed between his ass cheeks. Jude moans and grinds back against me. It's a workday, so we shouldn't linger in bed too long.

"Morning," Jude mumbles.

"Morning, hun."

"Someone's eager to get started on our wonderful weekend of debauchery," Jude teases. He reaches around to stroke my dick. We've been talking about this a lot, with the distance separating us. This is the weekend we go bare for the first time. No more condoms, except possibly to help my dick stay rigid enough to penetrate him.

"So eager," I agree, rutting into his palm. I wrap my hand around his morning wood to return the favor, reveling in the silky slide of his foreskin over the glistening head of his cock.

"Want to try something different?" Jude suggests with a wicked gleam in his eyes.

"What did you have in mind?" I ask. Jude lets go of me, encouraging me to release his dick. He moves to straddle my thigh and brings our dicks together. He rubs the slick head of his dick against mine, smearing pre-cum over both of us. I moan at the visual, reaching to add my hand to his. Jude stops me. "Let me."

"Okay." I've already discovered my dick is most sensitive near the base for now. Firm strokes like this are wonderful. The nerve connections are still healing, I'm still gaining sensation, but even if I couldn't feel a thing, this is incredible. It's still hard to believe I get to do this with my guy whenever we want.

"Just a second, hold the base steady?" he suggests. I do as he asks, the firm pressure of my hand on the base of my dick stimulating my buried T-dick. Yeah, this feels fantastic. Jude moves back enough to align our dicks with the tips mashing together. As I watch, he works his foreskin over the head of his cock. Then he keeps stretching it, working the edges over my glans, stroking the foreskin over us both. Jude jerks our dicks together within the tight slick sleeve of his foreskin. It's the single most erotic thing I've ever seen; the two of us joined together as one and I stoke the base of my cock.

"Fuck, Jude!" I try to hold still, so I won't fuck up the angle or hurt him by moving too much. "Hun, oh my god, yes."

Jude cuts off my excited sounds by pressing his mouth to mine. Our tongues tangle as he continues to stroke us with measured movements. He groans as he comes, the hot flood of spunk oozing out around my dick, coating us both. It's easy to imagine it could have been mine. Jude rubs the head of his spent dick over mine, smearing the mess around as I jerk myself to completion too.

"Good?" Jude asks with a satisfied smirk.

"So good," I agree, pulling him into a kiss. "I love you, hun."

"Love you too, snuggle for a bit before we eat?"

"Yeah," I agree, knowing it will be a short snuggle because he's a stickler for his schedule. We should get to work at a reasonable hour. He'll probably drag me off to do some sort of exercise at some point today, too. That's part of his routine, and our morning sex is going to make us too late to squeeze it in before work. That's fine. I've got plans to put in motion before we can spend our weekend of sexcapades lounging in our bed. I hate the idea of ever getting up when I'm all warm and loved up with my Jude in my arms.

All too soon, he squirms away to go to the washroom and test his sugar. Gui isn't home, as I expected. Jude and I eat one of his hasty healthy meals. Then we get ready for the day. Jude is faster than me, he waits on the couch for me to get dressed. He's wearing one of my t-shirts. I love seeing him in my clothes. Good thing too, because he is constantly swiping my shirts and stuff. It's the first Friday of the month, so I've got an adult sized dinosaur footie pajama on for dollar donation day at work. Not that you have to dress up to chip in, but I like that I can be silly like this, it's fun. Jude doesn't tease me about the outfit like my old roomies used to do. He's the one who got me the dino for my collection. It's got bright neon stripes, and even has a tail that sticks out behind me. That part makes it awkward to sit in, but I don't care. It reminds me of Jude and that's enough to put a smile on my face. Just when I think I can't love him any more than I already do, he goes and does something that shows how much he gets me.

We've got our first game session since my surgery tonight. I'm excited to play again. The gang might actually make it to the mercenary encampment to rescue the dragon prince at this session. Or they might get sidetracked yet again. Either way, it'll be a good time with my friends.

Fun, but no longer my reason for being. Not like when my dysphoria was at its worst as an adolescent and my characters were my sole outlet to be me. Now VentureQuest is just a fun game, not an escape from my reality. Something I enjoy doing with my best friends. That's even better, getting to share my love of the game with people I love instead of using it to avoid my issues and hold my depression at bay.

These days, I don't need an escape from my reality. I have an amazing group of friends to play with. My body fits. My boyfriend is there for me, even at my worst. And my dysphoria is all but gone now that I've recovered from the surgery. It's not like everything is magically perfect, but the crushing sense of wrongness has vanished. The constant niggling dread of never measuring up isn't there anymore. I'm complete. Or most of the way there. There's still another stage to the surgery ahead of me. The erectile device may need a replacement down the line, too, nothing lasts forever. I still feel lucky that everything is on the right track for it to happen. For the first time since puberty, I'm completely at home in my body, and that's priceless. And well, there is one part of my life I'm hoping will last as close to forever as possible.

The morning passes slow, the anticipation of the weekend making everything drag. *Battle Fox* released a couple weeks ago. It's a big enough hit that we're going to be making a sequel, but for now there's a bit of a post-deadline lull in my workload.

Jude comes and finds me at lunch-time. He links arms with me for the walk to a little bistro near the Granville Market where we grab lunch. There's only one component that would make my life more perfect. It seems a little silly, and if anyone asks, I'm going to blame it all on Jude being a major league sappy romantic. But the thing that would make it perfect is a promise that this thing between us is till death do us part.

It's probably ridiculous to do this in the public market, but where better than the place we went for our first sort of date? It's better than the club I took him to the first time we hooked up, more romantic. I joke about not being about the hearts and flowers, but the first time I got him a flower remains seared into my greatest hits reel of memories. I'll never tire of how he looks lit up with joy, so I'm going with it. Besides, this is totally going to make Jude swoon. Dino pajamas and all.

We get to the little florist shop where I bought him the first of the rotating neon bouquet he keeps in our room and grab a pink carnation. Jude chuckles as I go down on one knee to present it to him. He's used to me being overdramatic when I present him with flowers. Only this time, when he reaches for the flower, instead of giving it to him, I pull out the box with the ring his brother helped me pick. His eyes go wide, but he lets me take his hand to present him with the rainbow inlaid band.

Kneeling in the flower shop where we ended our first date has to give me at least a plus three to this charisma check. The most important one I ever hope to make.

"So, you know I don't usually do hearts and flowers, but you make me want to, Jude. Your smile brightens my day and I want to keep making you smile for the rest of my days. You're the only one I want with me in my blanket fort when I need to get away from the world. So, what I'm saying is, you and me till death do we part. You know. If you want," I say, getting self-conscious toward the end of the proposal. It's weird to say the mushy stuff out loud, but it makes Jude happy. He beams at me.

"Yes," Jude says without missing a beat. "I want that, you big dork." Jude hauls me up to my feet and kisses me, his entire body pressed against mine. This step would have terrified me with anyone else, but I trust Jude more than I've ever trusted anyone. He's already shown me he's there for better and for worse. I want to be there for him too, with all the romantic trimmings he's always dreamed of having.

There are people around us, watching the spectacle, but they don't matter. All that matters to me is Jude in my arms as he agrees to keep on sticking by my side through everything life throws at us.

Thanks for reading Charisma Check! If you enjoyed it, be sure to leave a review. The Table Topped series continues with Saving Throw, Errol's story, available at: www.amzn.com/B08SL3WF2Q

If you missed Paz and Gui's story, Roll for Initiative, you can grab a copy here: http:www.amzn.com/B08R6M1XBT

And for a bonus steamy scene between Theo and Jude, check out the files section of my FB group at: https://www.facebook.com/groups/alexsalcove

ABOUT THE AUTHOR

Alex Silver (he/him) grew up mostly in Northern Maine and is now living in Canada with one spouse, two kids, and three birds. Alex is a trans guy who started writing fiction as a child and never stopped. Although there were detours through assisting on a farm and being a pharmacist along the way.

Visit me online at:

http://alexsilverauthor.wordpress.com/

Join my Facebook group at:

https://www.facebook.com/groups/alexsalcove

Follow me on BookBub at:

https://www.bookbub.com/profile/alex-silver

Sign up for my newsletter for a free short story at: https://landing.mailerlite.com/webforms/landing/i2w6l7

And as always, consider leaving a review on Amazon or Goodreads if you enjoyed this book, reviews are of vital importance to independent authors, thanks!

TABLE TOPPED SERIES

Roll for Initiative Book 1 January 2021
www.amzn.com/B08R6M1XBT
Charisma Check Book 2 January 2021
www.amzn.com/B08R6J14VZ
Saving Throw Book 3 February 2021
www.amzn.com/B08SL3WF2Q
Critical Success Book 4 Coming Soon

Charisma Check

Gui's the best friend I ever had. I love him like a brother, too bad I'm falling for *his* little brother.

Jude is a walking talking temptation, everything I never let myself want. He's sweet as chocolate, wickedly funny, and he gets me. The sex, well, it's worth a repeat and that's something I never do.

When he visited Gui, I thought I could settle for a one night stand, but then Jude moves to my city to work at my studio. Gui gets him to join my gaming group and suddenly he's all I see. Now Jude's looking at me with hearts in his eyes and I'm terrified that I'm going to break his heart.

Charisma Check is the second M/M romance in the Table Topped series. It features Jude, a hopeless romantic with diabetes who makes animation and Theo, a commitment-phobic trans man with depression who runs tabletop games for his friends. www.amzn.com/B08R6J14VZ

CW: for severe depression, gender dysphoria, mention of past suicidality, surgical recovery, injection medications/needles (insulin dependent diabetes)

Saving Throw

Rene was my first everything. Best friend, first kiss, first love, first heartbreak.

Seven years after walking out of my life, they tear open old wounds with a single photo of a smiling little boy and the message they're coming home.

Mo has my smile and Rene's eyes. It kills me that I didn't know about him sooner. As furious as the news Rene kept such a major secret makes me, I want a relationship with my son more than I want to rehash old arguments. Besides, Rene has more baggage than the 747 they flew in on, and I swore off love the first time they left me heartbroken.

When I learn Rene and Mo need a place to stay while they settle into life in Vancouver, it sounds like a perfect opportunity. I've got a spare room. What better way to figure out co-parenting than living together? It's not like I'm going to fall for the ex who hurt me deeper than anyone else could. That would be ridiculous.

Saving Throw is the third M/NB romance in the Table Topped series. It features Errol, demisexual panromantic production coordinator who likes to be in control and his first love, Rene, a non-binary trans masc ex-hockey player turned coach. www.amzn.com/B08SL3WF2Q

CW: Past mentions of a physically abusive alcoholic parent and portrayals of trauma/PTSD related to that, secret teenage pregnancy and related gender dysphoria/difficulty with accessing medical care. Side characters struggle with infertility.

HAUNTASTIC HAUNTS SERIES

Dan's Hauntastic Haunts Investigates: Goodman Dairy (*Book 1*)

Dan's Hauntastic Haunts Investigates: Hawk Lake (*Book 2*)

Dan's Hauntastic Haunts Investigates: Ivarsson School (*Book 3*)

Drew's Haunted Hangout (*A Hauntastic Haunts Short Story 1*)

Rafael's Haunted Halloween (*A Hauntastic Haunts Short Story 2*)

Lee's Haunted Holiday (*A Hauntastic Haunts Short Story 3*)

Drew's Haunted Hangout

What if your imaginary boyfriend wasn't so imaginary?

Drew was no stranger to feeling ostracized from his peers. His obsession with the paranormal began young. When he befriended Toby, the dead boy who lives in his garage.

Drew was the weird unathletic kid everyone avoided on the playground. As a teen, he found understanding in an online community created by a paranormal investigations vlogger.

Falling in love with Toby only made Drew's interest in ghosts more intense. But when he discovered Toby's striking resemblance to an unresolved missing person report, he didn't know how to help his ghost boyfriend.

At a loss, Drew turned to his online idol for help. The truth could set Drew and Toby both free, or destroy everything between them.

This is a young adult paranormal MM short story. http://eepurl.com/dNcScQ

Dan's Hauntastic Haunts Investigates: Goodman Dairy

When ghosts reach across the veil, Daniel Collins is there to tell their stories.

Dan is a vlogging ghost hunter. He has devoted his life to documenting paranormal activity. In his converted van, he travels around the country exploring haunted sites. He loves the thrill of filming restless spirits.

Chad Brewer, skeptic, works for an insurance company. He doesn't believe in ghosts, but watching Dan's vlog is his guilty pleasure. The cute vlogger is accident prone. He has Chad's work extension on speed-dial. The two talk whenever Dan gets hurt during an investigation, a frequent occurrence.

When Chad loses his job for approving too many claims, Dan offers him a position as his personal assistant. The pair sets out to investigate a haunted dairy barn for the vlog's next video series. The catch is that they must live and work together in Dan's tiny traveling home.

As the paranormal activity at the haunted dairy ramps up, so does the romantic tension between the two men. Can the love between a skeptic and a social media sensation conquer a vengeful ghost?

Dan's Hauntastic Haunts is a paranormal MM romance between a gay vlogger and his trans personal assistant. Buckle up for a hauntastic good time.

www.amzn.com/B07YSV2ZNQ

PSIONS OF SPIRE SERIES

Shelter	Novella 0.5	February 2019
Bright Spark	Book 1	February 2019
Bold Move	Novella 1.5	February 2019
Keen Sense	Book 2	April 2019
Weak Link	Novella 2.5	June 2019
Quick Fire	Book 3	July 2019
Clear Sight	Book 4	March 2020

New Ground A SPIREverse daddy kink standalone November 2020

***

Links:

Shelter	www.amzn.com/B07NM9XL8K
Bright Spark	www.amzn.com/B07NZ8KPS6
Bold Move	www.amzn.com/B07YVGZXDM
Keen Sense	www.amzn.com/B07R6L8W91

Weak Link	www.amzn.com/B07T4J2LJZ
Quick Fire	www.amzn.com/B07VGTF3NB
Clear Sight	www.amzn.com/B07ZQP7BDS
New Ground	www.amzn.com/B08NHQFJDZ

Shelter

Family is what you make it.

Former foster kid and abuse survivor, Elliott Sheffield, lost everything when he developed telepathy at twelve years old. He's used to not relying on anyone. There are worse things than being lonely and alone, even for a psion who craves closeness. He has plans for his life and nothing can distract him from proving that he can succeed. That will show everyone who cast him aside. Especially his former best friend Caleb Gaetz.

Pansexual, poly, psion, Caleb is comfortable with all of those labels. Life seems easy for Caleb. He has a supportive family and a vibrant social life. The future will figure itself out. For the present he plans to enjoy his university years to the fullest extent possible. He knows his hedonistic tendencies irritate his former best friend, Elliott, to no end. He just doesn't understand why Elliott takes Caleb's sex life so personally.

When life throws them both curve balls, they must adjust their visions for the future to one that will give them both a happily ever after, or risk their plans falling apart.

This urban fantasy romance contains an open M/M relationship, mention of past abuse, and positive HIV status. www.amzn.com/B07NM9XL8K

Bright Spark

Sometimes growing up means giving up your preconceptions.

Aaron Anderson and Jake Matthews were childhood sweethearts until Aaron developed psionic abilities that turned both of their worlds upside down and tore them apart.

Six years later they reconnect when Aaron returns home to work with a youth summer camp affiliated with SPIRE. Jake is at the same camp, along with his current partners, to protest the organization funding it. Sparks fly when the couple reunites and Aaron discovers hidden abilities that bring him to the attention of SPIRE.

Aaron and Jake have every intention of seizing their second chance at love. But once more, forces outside their control are at play. And the organization Aaron believes in is at the center of events targeting vulnerable youth.

This urban fantasy romance contains M/M and an open M/M/M relationship. www.amzn.com/B07NZ8KPS6

www.ingramcontent.com/pod-product-compliance
Lightning Source LLC
LaVergne TN
LVHW091041080826
845145LV00002B/576

* 9 7 8 1 7 7 7 3 5 6 3 5 4 *